Lonely Traveller Part 2

Sereno Sky

Special thanks to my son Mark for the excellent proofreading and editing, and to my love Beata for all her help and encouragement. I would like to extend my appreciation to all my readers, whose encouragement has been vital in helping me to write my second book.

"Sensitive souls don't have it easy in this cruel world. They feel like their souls are getting trampled on in so many ways. That's why you see their eyes light up when they can caress a face or an animal, or breathe in the scent of a flower."

—Sereno Sky

Table of Contents

Chapter 1: Lost horizon

"I just don't want you to make a hippie out of our daughter, Bernardo."

There she goes again, I thought.

"I'm not trying to make something out of anybody, Anne; you should know that." I find that too many people like to streamline their kids into becoming what they have in mind for them. Instead, our passion should be to love them no matter what they decide to do. We might not always like their decisions or life-style, but we should respect, support, and be there for them nonetheless. We might have some fears about their future, as we'd want them to have a good life, but fear doesn't make a good guide through life.

"I will carry on telling her how I feel about the world, my ideology, and my morals. She needs to know what I believe in, as much as she has the right to know that from you," I continued.

Anne had become quite materialistic over the years and would buy all the latest gadgets for Jasmine, our daughter. I was quite the opposite; intent on trying to preserve a simple and non-materialistic lifestyle.

"But Bernardo, just the way you live, wearing your bohemian clothing, the meditating and praying you do, as well as the music you listen to, is enough to rub off on our daughter," Anne replied. She wanted me to change.

"Well, Anne, don't forget that until a few years ago you dressed this way too."

She kept quiet. I had hoped that she would keep at least some of her roots. We had been drifting apart from each other for quite some time. It had started out slowly, but by now it had built up into some very evident and major differences. It seemed our lives were no longer running parallel to each, but had started to split into different directions.

"I would like to watch the sunset down at *the rocks*. Will you come along?" She didn't want to. She hadn't joined me for a long time whenever I'd go there, though I would always ask her again if she wanted to come. It was all part of the changes she had been going through. I usually tried to sneak away from such discussions and confrontations, as they didn't seem to lead anywhere, other than to increase the aching gap which had been building up between the two of us.

It was rather chilly. During winter, the temperatures drop at night in this part of the world. During the day, when the sun is out, it gets hot, which draws many tourists to the various sandy beaches of this island. At night, one must have a jacket or sweater along. I was freezing; I had forgotten to take mine.

It was about 16 years ago that we had arrived on the island of La Gomera, after having left Europe as young travellers. La Gomera is the smaller neighbouring island next to Tenerife, and many still call it the "Hippie Island" to this day. The first tourists that had discovered this paradise in the late sixties were young travellers. They had come from the United States, Canada, and Europe, supposedly on their way east towards India and Nepal on the famous *hippie trail*. This place seemed somewhat off their route, but considering the beauty and solitude it offered, I could understand why people wanted to go there, far away from mass tourism. Some of these idealists may have initially discovered the place, and then told their friends back home about it. Quite a few of these tranquillity and nature seekers ended up staying there for quite some time.

Due to a lack of being able to generate enough money, and after having found out that Anne had fallen pregnant, we had decided to move to the island of Tenerife, in hope of being able to find some stable income to support our small family. A few months after our arrival, our daughter Jasmine was born. She was indeed my big sunshine, whereas Anne had lost a bit of her shine in my eyes.

I was observing the waves as they were caressing the rocks

below. I loved this place, and would come here often after work, sometimes just for a short while, so that I could get home to spend time with our daughter. Because of the Spanish siesta, one worked quite late into the night, so by now the sun had already disappeared. In summer the sun would set later, making it possible for me to enjoy many a sunset after work.

We had used to come here quite often with Jasmine, whom we just called Jasi. It was a hangout for the few hippies and alternative-minded folks that lived on the southern part of the island. We would bring our guitars along, as well as bongos, flutes, and other instruments. We often ended up jamming until late into the night, especially on weekends when no one needed to go to work the next day.

One of the aspects adding to the beauty of this place was its remote location, away from the hectic tourist resorts. You could easily get down to this retreat after work to find some peace of mind, or someone to talk to. We called it "The Rocks", and it was located at the very end of Los Cristianos, which was the town where I worked.

Los Cristianos had transformed throughout the years from a sleepy little fishing village into a buzzing tourist resort with endless apartment complexes. It wasn't a very charming place now, to say the least, but one needed to work where there was money to be made. My workplace was a small storefront with open doors, and I sat mostly in front and gave people information. The company was running a large excursion boat, taking tourists out to watch whales and dolphins in their natural habitat. Speaking five languages, it was easy for me to sell tickets to tourists from all over the world. I enjoyed being my own boss there, without having anyone interfering with my work, which I could do better than Pablo, the owner, who only spoke Spanish. It was still amazing to me how quickly I had picked up the local language without ever taking a lesson, but just by talking to people.

The sound of disco-music was streaming over from "La Roca", the open-air club. It didn't bother me. I had learned how to divert my attention from that and was listening to the waves instead. I'd noticed long ago that the mind, as well as the noise around, needed to be silenced at times. I would sometimes spend time meditating, tying to listen to that still small voice within me. Quite often, doing this had helped me find peace about my life in the past. That was when things had been running normally. Lately they hadn't, and I felt increasingly restless inside. This made it more difficult to just turn off and tune in, as my mind kept racing around after all kinds of disheartening thoughts.

I was thinking about my conversation with Anne today. It seemed as if we had arrived at a very difficult point in our lives. The situation having been like that for quite some time, one could in fact get used to it. Because of our daughter, and wanting to keep the status quo, I had often just swallowed our differences. We can get dull to reality, not wanting to rock the boat, because that could mean that some nasty changes might be needed. And who would enjoy looking forward to painful changes? I think that's why we often don't desire them in our lives; because we know that for things to get better, they might first need to get worse. We might even resist them, always looking for less hurtful solutions.

I heard people approaching and I noticed Birgit, the German girl. We had become good friends recently, after having seen each other regularly at this spot. She owned a small jewellery shop in Los Cristianos, selling her own hand-made creations. She would often be sitting down here after work, and sometimes I would see her putting together some bracelets.

"Bernardo!" she looked up as she saw me. "I didn't expect you to be here today. How are you? And how are Anne and Jasmine?"

I tried to hide the deep thoughts I had just been turning over in my mind. "I think they're fine. I'll be going home soon to find out."

She introduced me to her friends who had come for a two-week holiday. "We are on our way to La Roca, and I just wanted to show my friends my favourite hangout." They sat down and we got ourselves busy with some small talk.

After a while it seemed the couple were impatiently looking towards the place where the sound of the music came from, so Birgit encouraged them to go ahead and she'd join them later. It was easy to find the way to La Roca as one just had to follow the sound.

"Why didn't you go with them?" I inquired.

She looked at me with a type of hidden smile: "I didn't feel like it. And it's not so much my world anyways; I prefer staying here and talking to you. Or maybe listening to you? You seem to be in deep thought. I haven't seen you like this before."

"Well, sometimes life catches up on us," I mumbled.

I noticed that her smile had disappeared, and was replaced by an air of seriousness. I couldn't tell what colour her eyes were, as the moon wasn't strong enough to show. We hadn't conversed very deeply until now, but I always appreciated the air of silence that surrounded her. She wasn't very bubbly, to say the least, but that made her somewhat mysterious and interesting. And maybe also trustworthy, because people who babble a lot might do so about you as well.

"That's so true. We go through different stages. Sometimes life follows us where we want to take it, but other times it takes us on a ride. We may be in full control of our lives, but then something happens that shatters everything and makes us lose control. That can be very unsettling indeed." She hit the nail on the head. "I've had similar situations in my life, and those were very difficult for me."

"Yes, it's been hitting me with full force lately. I used to think that I had a firm grip on things, but during the past year I felt the reins slowly slipping away, and I'm not accustomed to this. It's been quite unsettling and frightening, and sometimes my thoughts even keep me up at night." I was surprised at myself for revealing so much to someone I barely knew. At the same time, I felt that she didn't want to take advantage of such sensitive information, but was sincerely listening and relating to her own experiences. There is certainly a difference in communicating with someone who cannot only listen, but also understand.

She was a couple of years older than me and had been living on the island of La Palma before coming here, until she fell in love with a local *caballero*, who wanted to move with her to Tenerife. Why she and her *caballero* were no longer together hadn't yet become a topic.

"Do you like your job selling excursion tickets?" Birgit asked.

"It's ok," I answered. "I'm selling well because of the various languages I speak. I also like the personality and ideology of Pablo, my boss. If people don't get to see the whales or dolphins while out on the boat, they receive a free ticket to go out to sea another day. I find that to be quite fair. He's not just *screwing* the tourists in that sense. Besides, I prefer people going to see the animals in their natural habitat, rather than sticking animals in a zoo."

This was a topic I was quite adamant about. "I have nothing against photographers taking photos or making documentaries of animals out in nature. There is certainly educational value in that. But I will forever consider it to be one of mankind's many horrors that animals are being caught in their wilderness, transported thousands of miles up north to cold climates, only to be put behind bars in some place called 'The Zoo'. That I cannot view as being educational for our children, but rather the teaching of human cruelty."

"I remember you told me something similar the first time we met. Remember?" Since it was one of my concerns, I was quite vocal about it, and would frequently mention it when this topic came up. "I'm glad that you found something to that you care about. I read some studies that indicate that especially dolphins seem to enjoy people coming over to see them."

"Anyways, to answer your question honestly, it's a job for the money. Easy to do, ethical enough to not feel bad about; but still a job, and not my passion," I concluded.

"So then what is your passion?"

I must have looked quite empty when I answered. "I don't know yet and I don't know if I ever will. How is it going for you?" I realized my answer was cut short, but I didn't want to reveal how much it bothered me to still not know where I was going, and what I was supposed to do in life.

"I've been doing well with my jewellery shop. I needed to adapt in my work since coming here, as most of the tourists aren't hippies, as you know. I changed my style of jewellery accordingly, trying to cater more to the needs of regular tourists, and I have been selling well that way. At least I make enough for a living."

I reflected on that for a moment: "I guess many of us had to adapt to new situations after the hippie movement came to an end. Sometimes I think that since we couldn't change the world, many of us ended up having to go along with it, sort of like 'if we can't beat them, then join them.'"

She looked saddened. I guess many of us felt a certain amount of nostalgia for that era.

"It's true, Bernardo, I've seen many of my former friends turn to materialism, like they would have all the catching up in the world to do. Buying big houses with swimming pools and fancy cars, forgetting all about the spiritual values they had once held dear."

I had certainly seen that happen as well. This wasn't the first such discussion on this topic I'd had throughout the years. I was thinking about my friend Eduardo from Argentina. He had been making little trees and other creations, using golden wire and fastening semi-precious stones onto them. He used to sell these beauties on the promenade where the tourists would pass.

After their second child was born, they had received some major financial gift from her parents, which they used to buy a large shop. From then on, all the products he sold were imported from overseas. The times of his own creativity were over, and now they were going after the big money. They took up a huge bank loan to buy themselves a fancy house with pool up in Arona. Our friendship had gone down the drain, as he was no longer hanging around with us, but got involved with more materialistic type of people.

I had noticed him change tremendously from the

simplicity he had exuberated before. He was now driving an expensive car and putting his money to use in various shady and non-shady business. When Anne and I had first arrived here on the island, he and his wife Maria had helped us move into a rental apartment near the place where they had lived. It was only a couple years ago that we had saved up enough money to make the down payment and move into our little house up in the hills.

We had been meeting up regularly while living almost next door to them, and would often go to some beach together with the kids, or come here to *the rocks*, and play music together. Sadly, since they had gotten their shop, they had started coming less and less. To have money, and to have a lot of it, didn't seem strange to them anymore, and it seemed they had gotten somewhat sucked in by the materialism they had once detested.

It was not that I considered putting some money aside for future needs and dreams as something inherently evil. It was the love of it, and the loss of ideals because of money, that I had a problem with.

Anne had gotten affected by this as well throughout the years. Lately, she had started to bring up the idea of wanting to build a large swimming pool in our yard, suggesting to take on another big loan for that, as well as for constructing an annex to our house with a bigger room for Jasmine, as well as a guest room.

Our house wasn't large; we had just two bedrooms and an office, but it was very cosy, and I had been working hard for many years to reach the down payment. For me this seemed more than enough, especially since we had already agreed that we weren't going to have any more kids. Whenever this topic would come up, I wasn't very enthusiastic, to say the least. I had no desire at all for further credits from the bank, and thought that I'd be glad if we were ever able to pay back the debts that we had already committed to.

"Well, Bernardo, I don't really know all you're going through right now, but it seems that the travelling days seem to be over for you, and now life has hit you straight between the eyes. Maybe you will be travelling more in other kinds of ways. This time around, they might not necessarily be physical places that you will be visiting, but places of great significance in your heart." She had interrupted my thoughts, transporting me back to the present.

"You're right. This is something I may need to learn now. I guess that can be quite a difficult process." And I wasn't looking forward to that.

She looked at me, and this time I thought for a moment that her eyes might be blue. Or maybe that was just because she seemed to have a hopeful and positive outlook, while mine seemed rather foggy and grey these days. It was getting late, and I realized that I had been so involved in this discussion that I had totally forgotten about wanting to help Jasmine with her homework.

"I'm going to look for my friends. Will you come over to La Roca with me?" she asked. I would have liked to, just to get my mind off my problems, but I knew Anne was probably waiting for me, and I didn't want her to worry.

"Perhaps another time; I would like to pass by your jewellery shop one of these days to see what sort of things you create." I accompanied her over to the open-air club and then went on to my car. Since Anne and I were working at different hours, we each needed a vehicle. I had found this little VW beetle, which looked very old, but was working quite well. Someone must have brought it down from Germany, and it obviously had been used by some interesting folks, as it was decorated with painted flowers.

Anne had insisted on getting a new car. She said she needed to start looking more professional at the yoga centre, because her boss, an English guy called Mat, had indicated that she might become second in charge soon. It was evident that she had to have a car for going to work and back, as going by bus was very time-consuming. But I wasn't hot on getting a brand new one, as it meant to take another big credit. To avoid conflict, I had ended up quietly agreeing, and so she got herself a convertible, for which she was very pleased. It was nice, no doubt. But it was again financed by the bank, and taking on one chain after another didn't seem very liberating to me.

She was still up and waiting for me when I got home. "I'm so sorry for being late. I went to *the rocks*, wanting to relax for a while, as it had been a very busy day at the office." She looked quite edgy. "Then why didn't you call me?"

I could understand why she would be upset. I hadn't planned on staying that long, but ended up being engrossed in this lengthy conversation with Birgit. I tried to explain it to her, but that didn't seem to help. She wasn't usually the jealous type, which made me wonder at times if she still loved me. There were a lot of things these days which made me question that. I couldn't even tell when exactly we had started to drift apart.

Soon after arriving in Tenerife and after staying for a few weeks at "Torres del Sol", we had moved out of those skyscrapers and into a lovely apartment up in Arona. As mentioned before, we had become good friends with Eduardo and Marie, and they had found the apartment for us. We were very thankful to move away from the busy towns and up into the hills. There were a lot of pensioners living up there, as well as many locals who worked down at the tourist resorts. Not only was it cheaper to live up there, but we usually had a little breeze coming in, which made living up there a lot more pleasant.

Jasmine's birth had gone very well. I treasured those early days, holding her in my arms or putting her to sleep on the terrace by singing to her. Anne and I used to be very happy during the first years of our relationship, and I would spend every free minute at home.

After Jasi had stopped nursing, Anne wanted to do more with her passion for yoga again. With the money put aside from my performing, she wrote herself into a yoga teacher's course up in Puerto de la Cruz. She would only return home for the weekends, as she needed to travel to the other side of the island. We still didn't have a car then, so she used to take the bus. When I went out singing and performing at night, I would bring Jasi over to our friends. It was a tough time. I often had to let Jasi sleep there, because by the time I'd finished singing she'd be fast asleep.

"We have it so good now, Anne. Remember the times we were living apart? It was rough. And now we have our dream, and are able to live in our little house away from things." I was trying to bring a positive spin back into our lives.

Anne looked at me, and I could see a lot of disagreement in her eyes. "Well, Bernardo, it's ok, but it could be better. You know what I mean." I did know what she meant.

"Things can always be better, and probably with time they will."

She didn't answer. She'd said it all before, and whenever we had this sort of discussion she would come up with her usual arguments: "We can have it now. We can get more money from the bank, so why should we be waiting for years?" I didn't know how to answer to that kind of logic; it was so different from mine.

I loved Anne a lot, and always wanted to avoid confrontation. Since she knew that, she would just remain strong in her willpower, knowing that I would eventually cave in and let her have it the way she wanted. In any relationship, this can gradually diminish the love that once was strong. And unfortunately, this was happening to us.

Chapter 2: Drifting apart

I brought coffee and a croissant to her bed the next day. There was a bakery at the entrance to the village, and you could literally smell the freshly baked goodies from our terrace. I would sometimes go there and get us something for breakfast.

"Oh, Bernardo, you're so wonderful."

I hadn't heard anything like this for a while, and was taken aback. I remembered the times when I felt she had looked up to me and whatever spiritual connection and experiences I'd had. That was a long time ago, but lately I felt that people who were successful materially speaking, attained a higher status in her eyes than me. I'd been having this conflict for some time now, between staying true to myself and pleasing her and her expectations. I imagined that it must have been a similar experience from her point of view.

We finished breakfast out on our terrace while discussing the day, and how we were going to get ourselves organized. I enjoyed the view from up here. Since our house was outside of town, we were surrounded by greenery and even a couple of fruit trees and an avocado tree. We tended a small vegetable garden, but time hadn't allowed for it to get bigger, since we needed to be quite involved in making money to pay back the loans we had taken.

Anne had to lead a seminar at the yoga centre, which was going to last all day. My office only opened at 10 o'clock in the morning, so I still had some more time on hand. After a brief kiss, Anne left, and soon after, I heard her drive away in her car.

Once again it had been a night without romance. I thought about the last time we'd had sex. I needed to think a long time back. It was that night after we had returned from a party that was organized by one of her yoga friends. She was quite tipsy after a few *screwdrivers*. It had been a fun night out, and Anne did have some interesting friends, some of which I had already met before.

Most of them were somewhere between middle and upper class, with many of them originating from other European countries. They had come to stay on the island to get away from the cold climate up north, and had opened various businesses here.

They seemed to be rather affluent, and well-able to afford the rather pricey yoga lessons and seminars at the centre. Yoga had become quite popular and trendy, and was no longer reserved just for the hippies practicing it on some remote beach. By that time much of the hippie lifestyle had become commercialized; with much of their original music becoming main-stream. It bothered me, but times had changed, and that's how it was now.

Anyways, that night after the party, we ended up having sex after getting home. At rare times like these we felt the harmony again which we used to have, and we seemed to be able to forget for a moment that our clocks were ticking differently, and that ever-growing disagreements had become our daily bread.

Maybe there was still some hope that Anne would cool it a bit and get back to more simplicity, I told myself.

But in fact, she was hoping that my clock would start ticking faster, and that I would enter this race whole-heartedly, without constantly trying to put on the breaks. Unfortunately, our hopes and expectations had drifted apart towards a point of no return. My personal happiness and peace had started to go down the drain, and I was feeling increasingly restless inside, with no clue on how to tackle this problem.

After work at night, I found myself wanting to go down to *the rocks* more often, rather than going home. My job didn't offer much time to think, and so I was thankful for this place where I could sort out my thoughts and hopefully get some clues to which direction my life should take.

I didn't find adding a pool and an extension to our house a totally weird idea, but I just wanted to go slow, saving up some money first, instead of plunging into more and more debt. I also wanted to enjoy the things we already had, rather than always thinking of needing more. I came up with a possible compromise as to how we might still be able to function and accommodate each other.

"Why don't we just pay back your car first, Anne? Afterwards we could start saving up for a pool," is what I suggested. I considered that to be a compromise, because in my eyes we wouldn't necessarily need a pool, since we had the sea nearby. But she just didn't want to take that slow route; she wanted it here and now.

One thing we did agree on had to do with Jasi. We started taking turns staying home with her, enabling each of us to have some time off so we could stay out longer. We would continue to spend our weekends as much as possible together as a family.

After work that night, I closed my office and went down to the sea. I felt a breeze of freedom as I heard a guitar while approaching. The waves were quite high today and splashing over the stones in great force.

"Bernardo, it's so good to see you!" It was Robert, another one of my friends from Germany. He was a musician, and had taken over some of my gigs when I had stopped performing.

"How's it going with your music?" I asked him.

He appreciated the gigs he had inherited from me, and said that people were still asking for me: "When is Bernardo coming to sing again?" Well, I did still sing, but mainly together with my daughter.

Throughout the years I had been singing for her; mainly before bedtime. I had composed some children's songs, which she enjoyed very much. She always picked the songs she wanted to sing with me. Sometimes I would sing her to sleep, or tell her imaginary bedtime stories about animals. Recently she had wanted to learn the guitar, and so I had bought her one for her 15th birthday. I taught her some basic chords, and how to keep a rhythm. By now she wasn't into children's songs anymore, and was listening to popular songs on her Walkman. One day I told her: "You can learn to play them too, they're easy." She looked both interested and surprised at the same time: "Oh really? Show me!"

I tried to make it a priority to practice with her as often as possible and she picked it up fast. She wanted to progress, and I would often come home and hear her practice the songs I had taught her to play.

Robert, or Robbie, as most people called him, was a nice guy. Whenever he made enough cash, he would go back to La Gomera for a visit. He had just returned from being there for a couple of weeks.

"How are the travellers doing over there?" I asked him.

"Wonderfully!" he replied. "Recently a lot of young people have been coming down from Europe and staying at 'Playa del Ingles', or at the 'Bay of Pigs'. The ones who can afford it are staying at one of the inns; that hasn't changed much."

I missed La Gomera and the friends we had there. We'd been so busy in recent years that we had only visited twice.

"Why don't you guys go back for a weekend, Bernardo?"

That was a possibility; going there for a long weekend with my family. I got all excited about it. Perhaps it would help Anne to reconnect with the simplicity we had both experienced while there, during the beginning stage of our relationship.

That night I brought my suggestion to Anne. "That's a nice idea. We haven't been there for a long time; we've always been so busy." The few times we had taken a break were mainly to visit our parents in Switzerland.

"Well, it's a good time to show Jasi where we used to live before she was born. When we went there last she was so small and probably can't remember much. And we could show her some of our hippie history."

Anne shook her head. "Oh no, Bernardo! I don't want her to get too much of that kind of history. It's fine to show her the places we used to stay at, but I don't want you to make publicity for the hippie lifestyle." I kept quiet, as I found arguing to be so unpleasant.

The following weekend we were on our way. Jasmine enjoyed the ride on the ferry, with the wind blowing through her hair. "If I look very closely, maybe I can see our house."

I remembered the last time we had been sitting on this boat. She was about 5 years old and was very excited then too. "Look! That mountain is so big and is white on top." She had been in snow before when visiting Switzerland, but she didn't expect there to be snow on this island. "Mount Teide is so high that there is always some snow up there," I explained. It's indeed an extraordinary thing to live in such a warm climate and yet have a mountain so high that its peak is always white.

Our friends, Maria and Domingo, were overjoyed to see us again. The small house we had lived in was now rented out, but they let us use one of the bedrooms in their own house. We stayed up a while, updating each other about our lives. They were amazed at how smart and beautiful our daughter was.

Since they still had the old guitar hanging on the wall, we sang them some songs we had learned together, such as "Blowing in the wind" and "Morning has broken". Jasi also played them some of the more recent ones she had learned, which they enjoyed very much.

After everyone, including Anne, had gone to bed, Jasi and I were sitting on the porch and looking up at the stars. "Why can we see so many stars here?" she wanted to know.

"I think there is less electric light around here as the island is not very populated, that's why it's easier to see the stars." She thought about that for a moment. "I think they have something to tell us, but I don't know what."

"They do, my girl. And maybe, if we remain quiet enough, we might just hear what they have to say."

"Really? You think so?"

"Well, all nature is trying to speak to us whenever we are willing to listen. I do believe that, yes."

"It's difficult to hear what they want to tell me; there are so many thoughts in my head," she sighed.

"That's why we need to learn to meditate, and be able to shut off our mind on purpose. Otherwise it always keeps us busy." I noticed her pondering that idea, before she asked: "Will you teach me?"

"Sure I will. We can do it right now; it's not complicated. Just try not to think about anything and listen, as if someone would want to tell you something important. You won't be able to pay attention to what a person's saying, if you have a thousand other thoughts racing through your head at the same time. Just imagine that if the stars would like to tell you something very important, you'd want shut off your many thoughts. People often sit in a certain way when they do this." I showed her the main position people usually use for meditation.

After sitting there for about twenty minutes in silence, she turned around: "They spoke to me! Shall I tell you what they said?" I was very curious. "They said that I should learn to listen more if I want to find my way in life." This brought a big smile to my face, as I noticed how much it meant to her to have heard something. It reinforced my view that we don't need to own much, or be rich parents, to help our kids to make it in this world.

"And what did they tell you?" she wanted to know. I thought for a moment. "They told me that you are one of them, and that I should be very thankful that you came down here to dwell with us."

She smiled. "Thank you for teaching me how to meditate. I love both you and mommy a whole lot." She gave me a big hug and kiss goodnight, and then went to sleep. I remained seated there with tears rolling down my face. I felt so much love and appreciation coming from my daughter, which made me forget all my problems, giving me a sense that it was worth it all, even the troublesome times I was going through.

The next day we went down to the sea to visit Vueltas, the small fishing village, and to have a swim at the beach there. We noticed a few gorgeous jellyfish floating between the fishing boats. I explained to Jasi that although they are magnificent to look at, we mustn't get close to them, as they can sting very badly with their long tentacles underneath the surface.

"They're splendid; look at those colours!" She had never seen one before. They're indeed amazing to look at, like a big bubble of pinkish-purple glass gliding on the ocean. They didn't seem to move on their own, but were peacefully gliding on the surface wherever the wind and waves would move them.

Later that day, I asked one of the local fishermen if he would take us along the cliffs with his boat for a few *pesetas*, and he agreed. We had a lovely boat trip along the same coast where Anne and I had seen dolphins for the first time. We weren't going out that far with Jasi, as I had already brought her a few times to see the whales and dolphins on the excursion boat in Tenerife.

Anne was quiet. It seemed like her mind was somewhere else.

"Look Jasi, this is the 'Bay of Pigs', where one can almost always find some young people." She looked very interested as she inquired: "What are they doing there?"

"They are celebrating solitude and being away from civilization. They live in the caves that the waves have formed throughout the ages."

"Did you guys stay there too?" came the next query.

This time it was Anne who answered: "Daddy would have liked to, but I was against going there. I think it's too dangerous as every so often rocks fall down, and sometimes the waves get quite high and flood everything."

Jasi looked concerned: "Oh my, these poor people. They shouldn't stay there!"

"They like to be adventurous and want to do something different. Nonetheless, your mom is right. It is known to be somewhat risky to be there, and that's why we didn't. We slept at a lovely beach inside some stone circles."

"Really? Where?" she wondered aloud.

"At 'Playa del Ingles'; that's where many youngsters are staying as well. We can go there tomorrow if you'd like," I suggested.

"Yes, I want to see where you guys were sleeping. That sounds like fun!" I was hoping that she'd never grow out of such enthusiasm and curiosity.

The boat moved closer to the shore, as our guide realized that we seemed interested in seeing the 'Bay of Pigs', as it was called. While getting closer, various people with friendly smiles were waving at us. It was quite amazing to see so many young people still following the same lifestyle as we had many years prior. We could hear the strumming of guitars, as well as the sound of drums and flutes. It seemed they were just starting a fire.

"They're preparing for the sun to set. Many young people enjoy celebrating the sunset." I explained to Jasi. Anne looked displeased; I could tell.

"I think that's really nice. I enjoy sunsets too. Last week I painted one at school". Now it was my turn to look surprised.

"You did? I'd love to have a look when we get back home. You used to always show me the things you made at school." She promised to do so once we got back. Maybe she thought it was not so cool anymore to show us parents the things she made at school; or perhaps she thought it might not be good enough.

"Why did you guys stop being like hippies?" Jasi turned around and asked. There was silence for a while. I didn't know if Anne wanted to answer that one, but I could see in her eyes that she expected me to be the one to do so.

"Well, people change. Many of the hippies started having children and had to take on a more settled and responsible lifestyle. But some are still hippies in their hearts."

She smiled at me and said: "And you still look like one with your long hair and funky clothes."

I took that as a compliment, while Anne seemed to be quite turned off by what her daughter had just said. After returning to the port, we were enjoying some dinner at one of the restaurants there. I explained to Jasi how I used to gather carob pods, painting and selling them to the tourists; and how her mom would make bracelets and necklaces, offering them to sunbathers at the beach.

"You guys were really adventurous. And what do carob pods look like?" she asked.

Since I knew where there used to be a carob tree in the vicinity, we passed by after dinner. "Wow, those pods are huge!" she said in amazement. I was pleasantly surprised to see that one had fallen from the tree and hadn't been picked up yet.

"Look, here's one!" I showed her how the beads inside make sounds like a shaker. She loved it. "It's yours. Maybe when we get back home I will paint it for you, just like I used to."

"That would be so nice!"

Anne kept quiet most of the time, and I felt like she was experiencing some agony inside. I just couldn't understand how someone would want to hide their past, just because they grew out of it. It almost seemed as if she was ashamed of ever having adhered to that kind of lifestyle in the first place.

"We have so many wonderful memories of this place, don't we?" I tried to get the conversation with her going later that day, while sitting at a beach café next to the small 'Baby Beach', where Jasi went for a swim.

"Yes, we do. It was a different time, and life was wild and free. But now we have responsibility, and a child. We need to get used to this new reality." She was right about that.

"I agree. There are always changes in life, nothing stays the same. Yet at the same time, I believe it's important not to lose touch with our roots and where we came from." She looked at me, but not with the same enthusiasm with which she had looked at me in times past.

"Look, Bernardo. I also know my roots; but now I have new friends who were not hippies, and they are responsible people who care for their children and want them to have the best." I was astonished by the tone of her voice. There seemed to be some implication in there that I didn't care enough for our daughter.

"I agree with the importance of caring for our kids, and I also want only the best for Jasi. That's why I had agreed to buy the house. I am working every day to pay back the credit." She didn't seem to be satisfied with my answer.

"Yet, we can do a lot more with our house and live a lot more comfortably. We both have a job now, and can afford to take on more credit, so that we won't need to wait for years to have our dreams. I want the best for our daughter. I don't intend for her to be some freak among the other kids. She shall have everything and every opportunity they have. I don't want her to be lacking anything just because we don't want to get more credit. Other parents are all in debt too, it's very common nowadays."

Occasionally, I would gather enough courage and stand up for my opinion, no matter what the result; and that's what I did now.

"Why should children be considered underprivileged if their parents aren't materialistic and don't own much? That's bullshit. It's so much more important to teach them to be kind, loving, and respectful towards others, to animals, and nature. We can show them how to tap into the real riches, such as the wonderful energy that nature extrudes, or being able to take in the good vibes the stars send out at night."

She didn't answer, but at least I had stood up for what I believed in. Since I was now in the mood for speaking up, I tried to add one more argument. "The world tries to entrap us with loans, credits and other snares, in return for their materialism. Those things are traps, and instead of life getting happier, you may find it getting more and more complicated. 'It's just a part of growing up to take on responsibility', they say. But one day you may wake up and realize that you have put on chains that you may have never wanted. It is far better to stay free and live a simple life, in my opinion."

Anne remained quiet, but I could feel that my arguments didn't do the trick. I had been harbouring some hopes that coming here might help her remember the modest life we had enjoyed after getting together. Regretfully, I began to realize that she had already made some choices in her heart; choices that I couldn't, and didn't want to follow any longer.

On our way to Maria and Domingo's place we passed by *Casa Maria*, where a lot of young people had been gathering at the beach front, drumming to the sunset, and with a crowd of tourists watching them from the promenade. Sadly, I couldn't enjoy the scene, as too much was going on in my mind. We sat down for a glass of wine, and I started a conversation about our friends whom we had gotten to know when we had lived there.

Ben and Claire had visited us a couple of times from Germany, and we had been keeping in contact with them through the mail, and had even called each other a few times. They had invited us to go see them in Berlin, but just as we were planning our visit, we received a letter from Claire explaining that they had ended their relationship. She said that Ben had become the head doctor in some private clinic, and this totally changed him. He just became too busy for her and the things she was interested in.

"Claire was always more the hippie type, not wanting to settle into a normal lifestyle," Anne said. "I guess such breakups can easily happen when people drift apart from each other and don't share common interests anymore."

I reflected on that: "I've read some stats recently regarding divorce rates being on the rise in the western world. Perhaps people feel freer to end a relationship that no longer seems to match. Maybe they can also more easily afford it than our parents or grandparents could, where usually only one of them would bring in a salary."

"That's right. And why should people even want to stay together when their interests have taken off into separate ways?" I knew what she wanted to say, but I guess it was still hard. One gets so used to live with a person and you usually still have some love for each other, despite differences. "I think people just need to learn to let go, Bernardo, and find ways to do it peacefully, and try to avoid negative repercussions this might have on their kids."

I was glad that our daughter wasn't listening to this conversation. She had joined the drummers, and I saw her shaking the pod from the carob tree, in harmony with the rhythm. It made me smile and brightened up these dark moments for a second.

Anne started talking about her job and how she'd gotten a lot more work since her promotion at the yoga centre. "Bernardo, I think this won't be easy for you, but I do need to let you know that Mat and I have gotten quite close in recent months." I didn't know why I wasn't surprised. Perhaps I had felt it all along; it had just never been spelled out to me like that. At the same time, I admired her courage to tell me.

"Thanks for filling me in, Anne. I much prefer learning of it this way than you hiding things from me."

I guess my openness and understanding encouraged her to tell me more, so she explained the history of how their relationship had developed. Since we had already detached ourselves from each other emotionally, it was slightly easier to take, without the feeling of being hit by a ten-ton truck. But it still affected me, as I now needed to start facing the fact that Anne and I probably wouldn't be staying together in the long run. There were worries about Jasi, and how she would be able to adapt to such changes. I was panicking inside. We agreed that we would continue our conversation at the next opportunity.

The sun had now set and it was time to go up to El Guro to Maria and Domingo for the night. Of course, I had a thousand questions racing through my head, while at the same time realizing that time would probably make a lot of things clearer.

"Daddy, this pod makes an excellent shaker. The drummers really liked it too and asked me where I had found it." I was glad to hear that she had enjoyed herself, and it gave me at least some peace of mind during this stormy night in my life.

The following day, after sleeping badly, we went to 'Playa del Ingles', the beach where we had used to stay after we had first arrived on the island. The stone circles were still there, and we noticed a lot of young people with their backpacks. They were sunbathing and chilling in between the rocks that are scattered all over this beach. I pointed out to Jasi where we slept inside these man-made stone circles, to be shielded from the sand, wind, and sun. She was fascinated. The same stone circles, and probably many new ones, were still being used for spending the night and for sunbathing.

"I didn't know that there still are so many young travellers," Anne said.

"Yes. Robbie had told me that many of them are still coming here from all over Europe, due to La Gomera's reputation as a hippie island," I replied. "Many of them stop at my office in Los Cristianos, asking me where they can get on the ferry that will bring them here."

Anne added somewhat sarcastically: "Well, just wait until they have kids too. Everything changes once people start having children." Now that I realized that I had lost her, I didn't need to hold back my opinion anymore.

"Just because the hippie movement disappeared, doesn't mean its ideals and goals have all disappeared too. One doesn't need a movement to have certain ideologies. I still know what I dislike about society, and the reasons for which I became a hippie in the first place. And I don't forget my roots so easily, just because there is no movement backing me up."

She didn't react, and I realized that there would be more precious things to do in life than trying to convince someone who doesn't want to understand.

On our return trip with the ferry I was feeling rather down. Jasi was tired from the bus trip over the mountains, and was sleeping on the bench next to us. Anne noticed that I wasn't in a good mood. "Bernardo, I know this is difficult. I believe neither of us is right or wrong, but it does seem that we have drifted apart in ideals. I want to embrace all that life offers, including a good standard of living, just like my friends and clients do, and without having to wait years for that. Whereas you seem to be satisfied with very little, and don't care to make the most of our situation."

I went over what she had just said, and it cut like a knife. I felt there was no appreciation for all I'd done to help acquire our little house. It seemed as if I just hadn't done enough. Then something came to mind that I had recently read somewhere: "Some people do have a love for each other, but end up being incompatible." It's a tragedy of life when this happens, and it hurts. Change is good when needed, but I could have done without all the pain involved.

Chapter 3: With a little help from my friends

A few days after our weekend trip, I found myself once again down at the sea after work. I had so much to think about, but I was trying hard to concentrate on the scenery instead. However, that just didn't work; I felt my heart burning inside. Some other people had come to observe the sunset, and I noticed Birgit sitting further down and meditating. I didn't want to disturb her. When the sun had set, she stood up and saw me.

"Oh, Bernardo!" she exclaimed. "It's great to see you again, it's been a while."

"I've been quite busy lately with family affairs." I told her about our trip to La Gomera as she listened attentively. Since I had her ear, I was explaining about Anne and I and the problems we were facing.

"Well, we all change," she said. "While some of us prefer to hold onto our old roots, some people find new ones and a different lifestyle. The tragedy is that this often drives people apart, and this seems to be what happened with you and Anne. I am sure it's a difficult time for both of you, and I can certainly relate to that." I was glad to be able to talk to her about this, as she seemed to genuinely care. "Come, let's go to Los Cristianos. I would like to show you my place."

She lived in the old part of town, on the second floor of an old house. It was a simple one-bedroom apartment in the same building that also hosted her jewellery shop. It was nicely decorated with art and a lot of different types of jewellery hanging on the walls; probably things she had made herself. After putting on some Pink Floyd and offering me some tea, I began to feel better.

"You seem to have the same musical taste as I do, Birgit."

She smiled. "I don't think I will ever not be able to listen to Pink Floyd. I'll probably still be listening to their music when I require the support of a cane. I seem to connect easily with their peaceful sounds, especially since the crisis I had last year," she said as her face saddened. I could see that she must have gone through some pain in her life as well.

"It wasn't easy when Pedro left. Not only emotionally, but he took a lot of my money with him that I had worked for. I hadn't expected that of him, and it was a big shock for me. We did have some difficulties in our relationship, and he would often stay away half the night after we'd had some argument. Then one day he was just gone with all his personal things, and he never returned. No explanation, and no sign. I later called his parents in La Palma, but they said he didn't want to talk to me," she explained.

I didn't know what to say, as I didn't feel I would be able to say anything that might be of comfort to her. Birgit added: "When someone doesn't want to live with you any longer, you must let them go. That's what I needed to do."

That hit me between the eyes. "You may be right, Birgit. But, when you have a child together, it all becomes a lot more difficult. Things take on a whole new dimension, and you don't even want to think about letting go, because it's tearing a family apart."

"That's true Bernardo. This makes my situation look a lot easier, and I don't know what I'd do in a similar situation. It's a lot more difficult, and probably a lot more hurtful as well."

She looked in my eyes as if she could see the pain that was burning inside. Her eyes were indeed blue, just as I had suspected the last time I had seen them in the dark. "Heartache and pain bring forth stillness, and a broken and meek attitude. That makes you being sweeter to others, more understanding and compassionate. I'm not promoting heartache, I'm still having to get over it too, but there is definitely some good in it."

"None of us wish to have hard times," she continued. "But sometimes they are necessary and are an important part of our spiritual growth. Maybe your life had been sort of easy, wild and free, and you could run away from problems and travel around." She paused, as she poured me some more tea. "Maybe you will still travel, Bernardo, but perhaps your travelling will be more towards the inside of your own soul."

I remembered her saying something similar once before, but this time around it made a lot more sense to me. But I was frightened by the thought of having to deal with pain, and anxious about what was going to happen. "Bernardo," she looked at me with compassion, as if she could feel what I was going through. "Do you pray sometimes?"

I was surprised for a moment. I had done often, especially since that experience up in the Swiss mountains.

"It's interesting that you would ask me that question. I have been praying, not as much as I used to, but I haven't stopped completely. I used to have a stronger connection, and I often felt like I heard a small voice guiding me. However, I haven't heard it so much lately. Life has just become too busy since Jasmine was born, and perhaps I had started listening to Anne a lot more rather than to that voice inside."

"Life sometimes *fucks* us up, and then we can't hear those whispers so well anymore," she said. "And then it's easier for negative vibes to get in and take away our joy and peace. It can become somewhat of a downward spiral."

I nodded. I was certainly no longer the happy guy I used to be. "But, last time that voice had told me that everything was going to be ok, and now things aren't ok at all." I guess I had just spilled out what had been bothering me, and probably the main reason why I hadn't been so much into praying anymore.

"I know, Bernardo, it can sometimes seem like that, but that's probably because of our concept of time. I do believe things will be ok, but sometimes they won't be so right away. It's in such times that we need to keep faith and hope, and try to understand the reasons why things are happening the way they do. There must be a purpose why these things have come upon you, and you must find out why."

"You're quite deep, Birgit."

I noticed the sad look on her face, as she went on to explain: "It comes from having suffered pain. Perhaps the pain you are suffering now will open new dimensions in your life for more compassion, understanding, and love. We're all at different stages in our lives. And just because you're now going through a difficult time doesn't make you any worse than the next person, it's just your time. I had mine last year, while others may have theirs in the future."

I realized that it was going to take some time to get my life sorted out.

"Well, it's still hard for me as well, but in recent months I have been doing better and finding some joy again in my life," she concluded.

It was time to go home. Even though Anne and I had agreed that we would each have time away every other night, I wanted to be there for my daughter when she'd wake up in the morning. Birgit gave me a warm kiss goodbye, and I left with quite a good feeling.

The stars were shining brightly on the way up to Arona, so I stopped the car for a minute to take it all in. I was breathing out a prayer: "Oh God, help me to manage everything. Please make things fall into place with Anne, and make it easy on Jasi." It felt like a huge rock falling off my heart. I guess that's what praying is for. I could hear that still small voice again, or perhaps it felt more like a whisper from the stars up, or like a breeze, although there was no wind: "*Trust.*"

The next day I left the office earlier to visit to Birgit's shop. I found that she wasn't a woman that could be figured out very easily. She had a very upbeat and positive nature, but could change instantly into a very serious and pensive mood. As soon as a thought would catch her attention she would want to go deeper with it, as if she was breathing it in and letting it fill her spiritual lungs. It seemed she would then add more air to those thoughts and breathe them out again, after having beautified them, like she doing with her jewellery. She seemed to blossom when she found someone who provoked her thoughts. Perhaps she had been alone with them for quite some time; that might be possible.

Her shop was filled with hand-made creations hanging all around, keeping customers busy browsing through to choose something. I imagined that the items under the glass table were the more expensive ones, which she would take out only if someone requested to examine them more closely.

"Do you have any friends, Birgit?" She didn't look surprised at my inquiry, and thought about it for a while.

"You know, Bernardo, the most interesting people come and go. I've made quite a few good friends in recent years, but they don't stay. At the most, they come for a couple of weeks once a year for a holiday. The people that live here permanently all work as well and don't have so much time. So, to answer your question: No, I don't have many close friends. Another problem is that I can't go visit my friends in Germany, England, or wherever they're all from. I need to be here or I will lose too many customers. When they come here they expect me to be available, and want to visit my shop to buy something. Some would phone in advance to make sure I will be here. Others send me a draft of their creation ahead of time, wanting me to make them a piece of jewellery from it."

"I only do the creation and the casting, right up to the process of moulding. I would then bring the cast to my good friend up in Puerto de la Cruz who is a specialist in melting and pouring. I don't do that here, and I've never learned it either. I only create and make the cast, or I do small repairs or adjustments. Some shops up in Germany and England ask me to make stuff for them, for example these here." She pointed to some leather bracelets and necklaces with *Fatima's hand*. They had small stones placed on them.

"Turquoise? It's so divine!" I commented.

"After creating the cast I bring them up to my friend's place. His name is Tom by the way. I place the stones myself. This one is turquoise, you're right. Here's one for you," she said, as she fastened one of her dazzling bracelets onto my wrist. Now my eyes must have been sparkling too.

"Thank you so much, that's so sweet. I'll wear it wherever

I go. It's such a gorgeous creation. This turquoise stone almost matches your eyes!"

"That way, my eyes can be watching whatever you do," she smiled.

"I somewhat envy people who are able to do what they enjoy doing, while generating enough income at the same time. You are truly blessed," I said. She knew that. "Yes, it's a privilege that not everybody gets. But in life there are different types of blessings. For example, I don't have a daughter like you do." She was right. We all have some gifts in our lives that other people might be longing to have.

"I'm not a professional jeweller, but people like my creations and that's what's important. Maybe eventually I may want to learn to do the mixing and pouring of the materials myself, but for now I prefer bringing my casts to Tom. He has learned it and does an excellent job. I prefer creating, that is my passion. There are good days and bad days at my business. There is a lot of competition with some shops selling similar products, but all imported from mass-manufacturers. Nevertheless, I make enough to live from it, and even able to put a little bit aside for whatever the future might bring my way."

"I used to paint carob pods and sell them when we were living over on La Gomera."

"Really, Bernardo? You paint?" She looked very surprised.

I explained to her how I enjoyed painting, but I had gotten into playing the guitar because I made more money that way. And now I was selling excursion tickets, which of course wasn't creative at all.

"Maybe you need to discover your real passion." She was right. I just hadn't found the time, as I had been too busy making money. And somehow, Anne had always managed to come up with new needs, for which I needed to bring in even more cash.

"I know. I see creativity getting lost when people need to work long hours at a job. There isn't much energy left at the end of the day to do anything else. I would like to get back into painting as a creative way to express myself. Playing music was never such a challenge for me. I could learn songs to entertain people, and it brought in the money. But I wasn't much of a composer and thus the creative side was missing. The few attempts I had at composing didn't deliver any satisfying results."

"It takes time to find out who you are and what you're supposed to do. Don't get discouraged about this and keep trying new ways." She began to close her shop and invited me for tea at her flat.

"Thanks for the invitation, but I would prefer to visit you again some other time. I need to go help my girl with some preparations for a test she has in German."

She kissed my cheek and whispered: "I have this feeling that there is a lot in you that needs to come out. I will pray for you that you'll find a way to express yourself."

Who knows? Maybe one day her prayers would be answered, I thought.

"I have an idea! Why don't you and Jasi come with me to Puerto de la Cruz next Saturday? I'm going to see Tom and bring him some casts and pick up some finished products. That might be very interesting for your daughter." I liked that idea.

When I got home I asked Anne about it, and she didn't seem to mind at all.

Chapter 4: When kids are no longer kids

That Saturday, we all drove up to Puerto, which is more than an hour drive on the highway. We decided to take the road over the mountains, which is far more picturesque and interesting. The road slowly winds its way up through small *pueblos* and pine forests. We stopped at one place as I had noticed some pine cones on the side of the road, and we got out of the car to gather them. They were huge. None of us had seen such majestic cones before. "I'll put them on my shelf," Jasi said with great enthusiasm. "They're gorgeous and I have never seen such big ones. The ones we had found up in the alps were much smaller."

On we drove through the lava valley right below Mount Teide. And although she had seen it all before, she was in awe each time we drove through there. "This looks and feels like visiting the moon, or some other planet. It always feels somewhat strange being up here," she said as she looked over the barren valley of lava rocks with no greenery.

"Maybe that's why people sometimes get to see UFO's around here. It's far away from populated areas, and there seems to be some special aura up here." She looked very intrigued by what I had just said.

"Please tell me more about it." I suspected that this wasn't a topic that had been broadly discussed at school, if at all, and so I felt it wouldn't hurt for her to learn more about it. "Have you ever seen one?"

I had, although I wasn't totally sure. It might have just been some strange military equipment flying over my head a couple of months ago, as I was sitting on our terrace at night.

"I guess I did, but it could also have been some secret plane that noone has heard about. It didn't look like a plane at all though, it was big and had a few edges; not round like they usually describe UFO's. It had absolutely no lights and moved very quietly through the night, making no sound at all. By the time I got over my initial surprise and called your mom, it had already vanished. I don't think the military has secret planes resembling what I saw, but I could be wrong."

"I do believe that they exist, Jasmine," Birgit said. "A friend of mine told me that they come here to gather energy from around Mount Teide, but they've also been observed above the waters between Tenerife and La Gomera". I'd heard of that before too.

"Well, I have an idea as to why so few people get to see UFO's and aliens," Jasi speculated. "The way some people treat each other, we can only imagine how unfriendly they might be towards unknown creatures. Maybe aliens are very gentle and sensitive, not wanting to observe all the suffering humanity creates. I would keep my distance too, if I were them."

"That's good thinking, my girl," I said, as Birgit and I looked at each other in astonishment at what Jasi had just said. I hadn't even noticed how smart my daughter had grown to be, and I was positively surprised.

"We don't know how many people actually get to see them," Birgit continued with the topic. "Maybe a lot than we know of. But since reporting to have seen one is a delicate issue, and many people might prefer not to talk about their experience. They feel that most people wouldn't believe them anyway."

"Yes, certain people might think you're crazy or strange if you'd tell them about such an observation. Anway, perhaps there's another solar system somewhere, with a planet like this one, hosting nature, animals, and inhabitants which are not intent on messing it up. And maybe those who want to live in love and peace can choose to go there when they die. The rest might prefer coming back here," I suggested.

"For the time being, I prefer to stay here and learn to play the guitar better, and to learn more on how to paint," was Jasi's answer to my speculation.

I was pleased to hear that she already seemed to have some goals for her life. "Proud daddy," Birgit said.

We carried on conversing, as we once again entered the pine forest on the other side of the island. This side of the mountain was much greener, like in certain parts of Italy or France. There was some fog, maybe just enough to keep the trees moist. The northern part of the island gets a lot more rain, that's why it's much more fertile.

We stopped by to visit the famous old tree, 'El Drago', and then drove along the heavenly coast line towards Puerto de la Cruz. It was such an enjoyable ride. We interrupted our journey once more as we noticed a farmer who had set up a table at the roadside, selling vegetables and fruit from his garden. They looked so fresh, and although he didn't call them 'organic', we certainly believed them to be just that.

"Look, Dad, the carrots still have some earth on them." We laughed.

"I don't think we need to worry about a little bit of dirt on the carrots we eat, my girl. It's like love-dust from Mother Earth. But what we should be worried about are all the poisons that humans spray on the ground in the form of pesticides."

Since everyone was hungry, we stopped by a roadside restaurant for some lunch, before continuing into town.

"It's good to have some ideas about which direction your life should take, Jasi. In a world where so many people need to work so hard just to pay the bills, it's important to find something meaningful to do beside just earning enough money."

"I know," she said with a serious look on her face. "I don't want to be rich, I just want to be happy. I've learned that from you."

"Oh, really? How?"

"Just by the way you live. You find happiness in all kinds of things: Carob pods, pine cones, sunsets, and in dirty carrots." We all started laughing.

"Yes, I find pleasure in things that can't be bought. That's probably why I can't really envy people with lots of money.

Because if you don't have much, then you are more easily inclined to find joy in things that can't be bought, like in nature and the animals, in good friends and good conversations, and in watching the waves of the sea."

Puerto is a classy old Canarian town with an ancient port and a breath-taking shoreline along the cliffs, with a continuous turn of huge waves splashing against the rocks. They sometimes crash so hard that you get all the mist in your face while walking up on the promenade. It's quite an event, with a lot of people just standing there and watching. When the waves aren't too high, the local youths jump into the ocean from the cliffs. The town itself has some homey plazas, and many original Canarian style houses with wood crafted balconies. I liked the place and always enjoyed going there.

One time, a few years prior, we had gone with Jasi to visit Lago Martianez, situated right by the sea. It boasts various big artificial pools in masterfully designed shapes by the famous architect César Manrique, who left his creative mark on many of the seven islands. The various pools are all connected, enabling you to swim from one pool to another without bumping into anyone. And although they are artificial, fresh water from the sea is pumped into them all the time. This, along with the careful planning and architecture, gives it a very natural touch. Jasi wanted to go there again, so we planned on doing so after our visit to Tom.

Tom's jewellery shop seemed to be a class higher than Birgit's and was in the centre of town. I realized by the price tags in the window that this wasn't the kind of shop I would normally enter. He seemed very excited to receive us, and he brought us right to the back of his shop where he had his lab. That's where he would melt different materials, pouring the molten mass into casts; either for rings, necklaces, bracelets, or whatever else one can purchase at such shops.

Birgit had asked him ahead of time if he would let us watch him for a while. She began to praise his work and how professional it was, and that she wouldn't get her jewellery done anywhere else. For just one moment I was hit with a touch of jealousy in hearing him receive so much praise from her. *I understand her appreciation for his professionalism, but isn't she overdoing a bit?* I thought to myself.

Jasi was fascinated by it all and asked Birgit if she would help her design a cast and create a ring. Birgit replied that she'd love to have her come over to her shop, and help her create one.

In the evening, Tom invited us all out to dinner at one of the restaurants by the sea. "I've heard from Birgit that you're still some sort of a hippie, Bernardo." I was surprised by his direct approach, but since he seemed to be interested, I didn't mind.

"Well, I still am; that's true. I needed to adapt my lifestyle, taking on more responsibility. But, as much as possible, I am still trying to preserve the ideologies of my youth."

"That's to be admired," he replied. "I was a hippie too, but look at me now. I think I might have adapted too much. I have my clients, and they don't want to see a freak in this shop. But even though I changed my appearance, I kept many of the beliefs I had when I young, and I still listen to Jimmy Hendrix, Janis Joplin, and most recently to Bob Marley."

"I guess what one looks like on the outside is much less important than what one believes in his heart." I think he liked my reply.

"Yes, and we also need some financial stability, Bernardo. This world is all built on materialism, and it's difficult to escape that."

"True. Nevertheless, the need for money applies terrible pressure. It causes so many people to have to do things they don't enjoy doing, or stops them from doing things they would like to do. Many idealistic people are never able to live their dreams because of lacking finances. On the other hand, quite a few idealistic people became very materialistic. I've been trying to prevent that from happening to me."

"I can relate to that, Bernardo. I used to be extremely poor, believe me. I had travelled to India, and then all the way up to Kathmandu. I wanted to find the essence of life, which I hadn't found at home. I had stopped my studies, even though I had been accepted to university. I told my parents that I wanted to go and travel, but for me it was much more than travelling. It was a spiritual search for something real; something that would stay in my heart, some form of *enlightenment* or *epiphany*, as they call it nowadays." I liked him.

"Birgit, you didn't tell me that your friend is a spiritual searcher. Why didn't you tell me?" Birgit looked at me with her usual sort of hidden smile.

"While on that spiritual search, one fine day I realized where I would need to find peace. I had gone hiking with some friends in the Himalayan mountains. But the higher up we went, the more it dawned on me that there wasn't going to be any point high enough to find that peace I was looking for. We needed to return anway, as we weren't experienced mountain climbers. We had made it up to this small Nepalese village, and it had a small temple. I thought that since the locals went in there to find peace, I should go in too. And while in there I suddenly became aware of the fact that there was a little temple within myself, right in my own heart. I was carrying that place of refuge and peace right inside of me."

We all quietly listened as he continued: "I prayed while in there. I guess my last prayers had been spoken as a kid with my mother. But now I formulated my own prayer to this invisible power, laying all my burdens down and asking for help and guidance for my life. And I felt a peace coming over me that has never left me."

"That's so beautiful!" Jasi burst out.

"I wasn't able to stay in Nepal, and I didn't want to become a monk in some monastery. I was running out of money and started making some simple jewellery to sell to tourists, but it was difficult to stay afloat financially, since most of the tourists in those days were young travellers from the west, like me, who didn't have much money either. After much contemplating about what to do, I ended up going to the next German embassy to ask for help, and they gave me the money for my trip back."

"That sounds fascinating, and will provide
for your kids, if you will ever have any," I sugg
out in laughter.

"Once back home, I knew that my passio
and I started to work at a shop. A few ye   ᵘ, ᵘ⋅ᵗᵘᵗ
checking out the situation here, I decided to come to Puerto
and open my own business, and it's been going very well. The
biggest joy for me is that I was recently able to buy a *finca* up in
La Orotava. It's an exquisite place: a small house which I've
been working on renovating, with a big garden around it. I have
been cultivating my own vegetables and fruit, and that has
become my passion, apart from my business."

Another one who has found his passion, I thought to myself.

"I'm so glad for you! That sounds great. I'm still looking
for my creative passion, but I do have a golden treasure, and
she is my passion." I turned to Jasi, who was leaning her head
against my shoulder.

"And you are my treasure." She was listening attentively to
the conversation we were having.

"See, you're rich, Bernardo. Just being thankful for what
we have makes us open to receive more. I'm sure you will find
your passion as well." He was probably right, and I liked his
positive outlook. Life has a way of bringing things at just the
right time.

"Yes, I do believe in Karma. Instead of taking our
frustrations over some belated dreams out on others, if we stay
kind instead, then our dreams might just come true," I
concluded.

"I believe in that too. And what do *you* think about the
hippies?" Tom directed the question at Jasi this time.

"I think they are fascinating. I don't see many these days,
but the ones I get to know, like the three of you, seem to have
benefitted from a positive influence on your lives. I like my
dad's ideas. We've been having very interesting discussions
lately. I'm sure the desire for love and peace hasn't ended with
the hippies. The world still needs people who believe in those
virtues."

'Yes, you're lucky to have a father who has this kind of ⸜ackground. And what are your plans regarding the future? Do you already have some?" Tom continued. She was contemplating this for a moment.

"I'd like to do something creative, like you guys do. I have many extraordinary pictures in my mind from all the things I see in nature. Sometimes I feel like I need to find a way to put them down somewhere to make room for more. My favourite class at school is art."

"You should certainly pursue that," Tom said. "But, you must work hard if you want to make a living from it. It took years of hard work to get this shop to where it is now, and to be able to sell enough so that I can live from it."

It started to get late, and we still wanted to go and cool off in the Lago Martianez.

"I hope you'll come again soon. I would like to show you my *finca* next time. I have some interesting plants in my garden. I think you'll like it, Bernardo," Tom said as we hugged goodbye.

After our swim, we drove back home, this time on the highway. I was glad we had taken Jasi with us, as she had experienced a very interesting day.

"I had such a wonderful time. Thanks to both of you for taking me along." It was nice to have a daughter who showed appreciation.

After driving her over to visit one of her friends, Birgit and I went for a drink at a nearby café by the sea. "You have such a gorgeous daughter, Bernardo! Not only in her appearance, but also in her attitude, personality and intelligence."

"Yes, I am indeed a blessed man. I was quite surprised today about her positive outlook on life. I've just been so afraid that the disharmony between Anne and I might be having negative effects on her. Not to speak of how she might get affected should Anne and I depart from each other." Since that thought had been bothering me, it was probably time for it to come out in the open.

"Well, Bernardo, just go with the flow, and everything will

work out fine. Don't worry about it. You will cross that bridge when you get there. Just *trust* God that everything will work out." Birgit affirmed. There it was again: "*Trust*".

"I'm scared about what the future holds. I would like to see changes in my life, but at the same time I'm dreading them. I'm scared of the consequences, especially the hurt it may cause Jasi." I was fishing for some positive outlook on my situation, and sure enough, Birgit gave it to me.

"I've read somewhere that pain is the fire we must go through to be healed. So instead of resisting it, and trying to hold on to that which won't come back, you might want to consider jumping in there and flowing with it, so that this situation in your life can accomplish its purpose. However, you're still fighting it, that's what makes it so hard and confusing."

She paused for a minute. Maybe she felt a bit uneasy about giving me so much advice, but I needed it. "I'm not suggesting to embrace pain as you would a lover. But at least embrace it as a companion who is there to teach you."

"It's not easy and you must wait for the right moment. If you'd try to work things out by yourself, you might make a mess. Let the wind blow when it blows, but don't start a tornado yourself. Let it unfold before your eyes, and then things have a chance to work out without some big storm."

That sounded like very wise advice indeed. "Thank you so much, that really helps." I could see in her eyes that she felt for me. She was indeed a compassionate and understanding person, and I appreciated her a lot for that.

"Maybe you prayed, and I might be part of the answer."

She was indeed. I realized that I should never be ashamed to pray and invoke some help from the universe, to assist me when things just got too dark. One could try to do without such assistance too, but I saw it work for me every time. Maybe one reason why we often won't pray is because we consider it to be a sign of weakness when calling on help from higher powers. It could be a form of pride, thinking that we should be able to manage everything on our own, without intervention from an outside source. I could certainly see that part of my prayers had already been answered in getting to know Birgit.

We had been developing quite a strong friendship during the past few months, but we hadn't gotten romantically involved. Things just didn't seem to lead that way, although, I must admit, I liked her a lot. Yet, I got this feeling that she looked at me more as a friend, rather than a possible lover. I hadn't been receiving any vibes that would indicate that her emotions were awakening for me in a romantic way. Perhaps she was ready for that, which was fine for me, as I presently had other problems at hand that needed to be sorted out.

After bringing her home, I went to pick up Jasi. It had been a very eventful and pleasant day for the both of us, filled with numerous new thoughts and impressions.

Chapter 5: Spiritual conversations

On Monday, after work, I met Birgit at *the rocks*. She wore a tie-dyed dress which looked very good on her.

"That dress looks gorgeous on you! I like tie-dyes, especially those in pastel colors. I prefer them to the bright ones," I remarked.

"Yes; I don't like colors that scream at me either. I made the design and then tie-dyed a couple of them. For a while I even thought of selling them at my shop, but then it might start looking too much like a bazar, and my customers aren't used to that. Besides, my biggest passion is jeweler. But what I'd been contemplating for a while now is adding an art gallery to my shop. There would be an empty room for that next to my shop which I'd be able to rent. But I'd need to find the right kind of art first, something that would suit my concept."

Robbie arrived with his guitar and joined us, while Birgit lit up a joint she had brought along. It was nice to see him again, as the last time we'd met was before my trip to La Gomera. For me, having these invaluable people around felt so much like having a family. The sun was setting, leaving behind a warm red glow on the horizon. I felt as if the sun's comforting energy continued to flow across the Atlantic Ocean, even long after it had already disappeared.

"That would be nice to paint." I was just sort of thinking out loud. "The good vibes the sun sends out, even when it can't be seen anymore."

"You should paint it. You really should!" Birgit said enthusiastically.

"That's such a lovely thought, and it would make an exceptional painting indeed." Robbie seemed to be quite turned on by the idea as well. "Bernardo, if you paint that, I will buy it from you. Maybe I would get stoned just looking at it." We all started laughing.

"I'll get some material tomorrow to start my first painting. I can't wait," I said. They both encouraged me to do so.

Robbie commented to Birgit: "That stuff you brought is good. I don't smoke that often, but tonight's a good night."

"It is a good night indeed. I have found it better not to touch that stuff when I'm down or depressed, it tends to increase negative vibes, and worries can grow in size," I mentioned.

"I guess we learned that over the years; that's why we enjoy it more when we do consume some. Too many people use it for any occasion, without checking whether their soul is ready or not. It does open you to good vibes, but it does so also to bad ones. It has a lot to do with the mood you're in when taking it," Robbie agreed.

Birgit leaned her head against my shoulder as we listened to Robbie's version of "Stairway to Heaven", which matched our general mood so well at this moment. As more and more stars appeared, they continued to reflect in their own modest way a few rays of all that light that had disappeared with the sun. "How wise and eternal they seem, as if they'd know exactly what is going on down here," Robbie marveled, while taking in another smoke.

"Bernardo, how far do you think all of that goes? I mean the universe?" I'd heard that question quite a few times in my life.

"I think there is a lot more out there than we think, including other forms of life. Believing that there would be nothing else out there is like being born in prison, thinking that these walls all around must be all there i"Maybe we'll become a star in the sky when we die," Birgit whispered.

"You? Definitely!" I whispered back. Robbie started playing some soft Bob Marley tune, while I thought more about what might become of us once we die. "Every little thing is gonna be alright," we started singing along.

"It's possible that when flowing out of our bodies we'll

change and become part of that universal energy manifested in nature, the elements, and the universe. I believe we're already part of that energy now, and as Einstein said: 'Energy cannot be created or destroyed; it can only be changed from one form to another'," Birgit continued the topic.

"Yes, and maybe we'll be able to roam around and discover much of what we hadn't been able to understand before; getting to know some of the hidden secrets behind the scenes. Maybe we'll be able to choose where our spirit would like to dwell next, if that isn't already planned. If I were to choose, perhaps I'd become a cannabis plant. They're gorgeous!"

"Bernardo, you'd certainly make a nice piece of *weed*, I'm sure. You'd get us tremendously high." Robbie stopped playing, and we all laughed.

"That's an intriguing idea," Robbie continued, deep in thought. "I wouldn't want to come back here in human form again; it's all too selfish for me as people only look after themselves. A minority of people own most of the money in this world. How could that be just and fair?"

"It's certainly not. Nevertheless, I don't believe in a revolution of guns and violence. That tends to only make matters worse, with people being used on both sides of conflicts for the political interests of a few," I responded.

"That's true, Bernardo. Whenever a corrupt political system was overthrown, most new political powers became just as corrupt as the previous ones. Couldn't there be a better way to usher in more justice and peace?" Robbie questioned.

"In that sense the hippie ideology was totally harmless and peaceful: That mankind should love each other, without there being discrimination against anyone, respecting the environment and all living beings. And helping one another instead of causing harm, making sure that people wouldn't need to die of starvation or war. That attaining spiritual riches was more important than joining the race for materialism. I don't see anything weird in that kind of thinking."

Robbie agreed, and added: "I admit that consuming too

many drugs was a problem for some, but maybe we were just trying to stay high instead of being so low."

"Well, we are sure flying high tonight and it feels so good," Birgit said, laughing, and her dreamy eyes looking very sparkly: "I love this conversation."

"It all sounds nice, but at the same time somewhat unrealistic and utopic." I didn't mean to put a wet blanket over all these hopeful ideas, as they belonged to the very roots of what I believed in.

"But Bernardo," Birgit interjected, "it's still better to entertain ideas for a better world instead of just accepting things the way they are. I agree that looking at all the chaos and injustice in the world can be utterly depressing. There are way too many negative vibes out there. But to help preserve our sanity we can't dwell on it too much. We must seek the good vibes of nature, purity and spirituality. That's not being selfish, because the world needs people who can still walk around with a smile."

"I agree with you, sweet lady. The utopic ideas we have might be the standard we'd like to see in the world, but it's so far from it. Maybe that's why some coined the hippies as *escapists*, because we had a problem facing that kind of bullshit. It's very difficult to present new ideas to a world that is so set on keeping true to its course of self-destruction. Perhaps one day we might need some aliens to come to our rescue."

"Aliens, come and help us!" Robbie jumped up and shouted out into the sky. We all chuckled, but not in a demeaning way.

"What if they heard you, and you will be whisked away one day, would you like that?" Birgit asked.

"Well, it might certainly be a very adventurous and interesting experience."

"Yes, especially if they'd come with good intentions to want to help us out," I added.

Birgit wavered: "I don't think I'd be ready for that. I have a jewelry shop, and all my clients. Maybe later in life I might feel more ready for such new friends."

These interesting thoughts finally left us in total silence. The disco was closed today, and except for the waves gently splashing against the rocks, there was no sound.

Robbie interrupted the waves: "Nights like these are unforgettable. They settle in your brain and heart. These are the memories we will feed on in dark days, when life might not be so friendly to us."

"And maybe some beautiful new memories are meant to replace old ones that we might not want to think about too much," I added.

"Yes, those memories. Some are worth looking back on; others cause more pain and distress."

I noticed a certain air of sadness in his voice and on his face. He must have had some painful experiences in his life as well, but I didn't think he would want to talk about those right now. Birgit, who was usually the rather quiet type, seemed as though she had just been waiting for the right kind of thoughts to trigger hers to come out and dance.

"Time runs like sand between our fingers. We look back at photos and writings, and wonder at how far we have gotten since then, and how much has changed. Sometimes we regret not having lived that time more intensely, nor taken in more to bring with us into the future. Yet we can still do that now, it's in our hands."

"This reminds me of my dog," Robbie sighed in a sort of nostalgic mode.

"You had a dog, Robbie?" I questioned.

"My last girlfriend and I had a dog together; his name was 'Stoned.'" We laughed about the name. "She took him back to Germany when she left. Of course, she was the one who had brought him in the first place, but he had become my dog as well. We had gotten very attached emotionally. It was almost more difficult for me to have him gone than my girlfriend leaving, because in the end she and I didn't really get on well with each other anymore," he explained.

"Sorry to hear that, Robbie." We both looked at him with empathy.

"Dogs only live to be about fifteen years old," Robbie continued. I could see in his eyes that he was still sad about the departure of the dog. "Maybe that is why they live so intensely. When I would come home he would be so thrilled, jumping up and down, wagging his tail and making sounds of joy. I wish we were all a bit more like dogs. I'm sure you've heard that saying before: 'Don't behave like an animal.' The older I get, the more I wish we would, and that we would stop behaving like ugly humans who destroy each other and the world."

"That is so true! Animals are very sensitive creatures," Birgit added. "Some humans are that way too. I believe sensitive people generally live more intensely."

"Yes, I believe they do," I contemplated. "Sensitive souls don't have it easy in this cruel world. They feel like their souls are getting trampled on in so many ways. That's why you see their eyes light up when they can caress a face or an animal, or breathe in the scent of a flower."

"Beautifully said. Yes, we must live each moment passionately. One day we might look back and think: 'Wow, those days were great! I lived, and I lived fully. I listened to good music, watched magical sunsets, had a blast with nature, and I was dancing in the rain."

"That's right, Robbie! Each day is one less on our list. We often let too many days pass without celebrating them. We need to start celebrating now, even if just with a jump in the air," I agreed.

Robbie jumped up again, screaming out: "So glad to be alive!" He had such a good sense of humor and could turn even the most serious conversation into some laughter.

"Along with this, there also needs to be a good portion of hope for what's to come," Birgit continued. "It is so much better to have dreams for the future, rather than nostalgia over the past; because dreams can still materialize, whereas the past is forever gone. But sad things do happen at times to deepen us, to make us more aware of the beauty of simple things, or to give us a much broader understanding for people who have difficult times. If everything would always go well for us, we wouldn't even be able to understand them."

"Yes, Birgit, like some of the troubles I've been having lately, they've certainly been helping me to become more awake spiritually. Sometimes things happen to people at a certain time in their life, and they suddenly become deeper and more interested in spiritual values. Nature and the clouds suddenly take on a whole new meaning."

"Oh man, this is heavy stuff! A lot of food for thought for these coming days," Robbie resolved while getting up. "I've had so much input, I need to reflect on all that, and learn to live more intensely."

"So must I. To top it off, I have a daughter who is growing up into a smart and rather spiritual teenager. I need to adjust to that and stop treating her like a child. I have other issues in my life as well, but this evening has done me a lot of good. Thank you both for such a wonderful time. You're both so sweet, and I am very thankful to have found friends like you". They both gave me a big hug.

"You'll manage just fine. You're a wonderful dad, and your daughter can be proud of you!" Birgit said, accompanied with a kiss. *What could be more precious than having friends like that? I* thought.

Chapter 6: Out of pain comes creativity

The next morning, after getting up late, I needed to hurry to the office. I had newfound energy, and wanted to be sure I'd close the office in time to be able to make it to the paint shop. I bought some regular paper for drafting, canvas, oil paint, turpentine, brushes, a palette for mixing the colours, and an easel.

That evening I was working on painting the previous night's sunset, which was still so ingrained in my heart and mind, when I was suddenly reminded of Jasi's painting.

"Would you show me that painting of your sunset? I would so much like to see it." She brought it to me. "Oh wow, that is gorgeous! Where is that?" She looked at me, hoping I'd understand.

"It's nowhere, or maybe somewhere. The teacher just asked us to paint our favourite theme, and I do watch the sunset quite often on our terrace."

"You do?" She nodded. "Of course I do. You just haven't noticed; you've been too much into your problems." That was hard to take, but it was true.

"You're right, my baby, you're right. I'll try to do better," I offered.

"Perhaps, if you have problems, you should get them out of the way. Then you can notice more what's happening around you."

I could only bow to such wisdom, and quietly think about how to go about doing that. There was no justification needed, it was time to face the facts.

Anne came home and looked at my draft. "Psychedelic stuff, right?"

"I'm just trying to start painting, and I'm working on that

sunset from last night," was my reply. I didn't expect any encouragement from her these days, and so I wasn't disappointed.

Jasi joined in: "But Mommy, it's really nice. And I like those pastel colours he's using." It was nice to see my daughter come to my defence.

I had been waiting for a weekend without clouds to take Jasi and Anne up to Mount Teide. Anne and I had agreed that we wanted to take some time together to explain to our daughter what was happening with us as a couple. We felt that combining this with a family excursion might make it somewhat easier for her. The following Sunday the weather turned out to be very clear and fair, which is important for the view. On a clear day one can see all or most of the other islands from the summit. We drove up to Las Canadas, which is what this moonlike plateau is called. There had been several eruptions of the volcano, the last one having occurred in 1909. We parked our car at the entrance to the gondola, and took the eight-minute ride up the mountain.

"Look, I can see La Gomera!" Jasi shouted out.

At 3718m, Teide's peak is Spain's highest. Luckily enough there were no clouds today, so the higher we went, the better we could see some of the other islands that form part of the Canary Islands archipelago. Jasi had been in snow during our visits to the grandparents in Switzerland, and we had taken her sledding and ice skating several times while there. Yet to touch snow here on this island was a whole different feeling. Close to the ocean where we lived it was pleasantly warm all year, and some call Tenerife the island of eternal spring. She started throwing snowballs at us as soon as we got out of the gondola. We needed to walk further up the mountain to reach the peak, and it was from up there that we had an overwhelming view.

"Which one is Gran Canaria?" Jasi wanted to know. She had been there with her school class for a week.

We could also see Lanzarote, where we had been for holiday a couple years ago, just before I had started my job at the excursion office. We all had enjoyed our time there; the island has so much to offer.

"Remember the trip to the volcanoes of Lanzarote? If there were any snowfall there, it would surely melt. The earth we touched on top of the volcano was so hot," she recalled.

It was rather chilly up there, and we were glad we had brought our sweaters along. We sat down on some rocks and enjoyed the breath-taking view. How amazing it is to get up so high, and see things as you normally only do from an airplane. I wasn't looking forward to explain to Jasi about Anne and I. However, such is life; one needs to take the bitter with the sweet. I had been so anxiously dreading this moment, fearing to hurt her and her feelings. I informed her about our growing apart in the past years, and I tried to observe the reaction in her eyes. I couldn't recognize any feeling of surprise in them, but I did notice a big sadness that cut my heart to bits and pieces.

"I've noticed how you guys have only been kissing and hugging me, but not each other," she said somewhat matter-of-factly. "If you don't love each other anymore, you shouldn't stay together." Now I probably was the one who looked surprised. She continued: "I just hope it won't be as it was with some of my friends whose parents separated. They're not even talking to each other anymore, and are waging some sort of war over who's right and who's wrong, over finances and possessions, and who should be able to see their child and when."

Anne and I looked at each other. Now it was her who started explaining, trying to put our daughter at ease.

"We get along fine; we just have different ideas about life. We don't fight about it and are both interested in finding peaceful solutions." She paused for minute to let her digest all of this. "We won't stay together, Jasi. At this point we don't know how things are going to develop, but neither of us is going to take off to parts unknown. We are not at war and want to stay friends."

She seemed somewhat relieved to hear that. "I like that. You remember when the parents of my friend Anna split up, and then her father went to England while she stayed here with her mom? Now she hardly ever sees him anymore." Jasi burst out crying. We put our arms around her. All her frustration and disappointment came out.

"Can we still make some excursions together, just the three of us?" she questioned. We assured her of that, and she seemed to brighten up a little.

All in all, I was surprised at how understanding she was of the situation; although I'm sure in her heart it must have been a big disappointment to her. Most kids in that kind of situation usually hope for their family to stay together, and for things to somehow work out, without the painful splitting up. Kids will probably never fully understand such developments until much later in life, when they themselves might encounter similar problems, like relationships falling apart and other such challenges in life.

It was important for Anne and me to provide the emotional stability, and to make it as easy as possible for Jasi during this time. I was glad that I had started getting into playing music with her. Anne had been spending time with her as well, taking her along to some of the yoga classes she was teaching, and on various walks and talks. They had a very good relationship, and I was thankful for that. It didn't matter to me that she seemed to be closer to her mom, entrusting her with more of her *secrets* and things she was going through. If anything, I was glad they had a strong and close connection.

All in all, the day wasn't as tragic as I had anticipated, and it seemed like Jasi had been somewhat prepared for our announcement and had taken it quite well.

During the next few days I continued working on my painting, until I felt there wasn't anything I could improve on it anymore. Jasi loved it. "This is fantastic, Daddy. I like the energy I can feel from it, through those warm colours spread out over the sea and in the sky. Does it have a title?" she wanted to know.

"I think I will call it 'After the sun is gone', and I will give it to Robbie for his birthday."

"Oh, I'm sure he would like that. You should show it to

Birgit too. Why don't we invite her for dinner?" she suggested. That was a good idea.

Anne didn't want to be there when she came over and had gone out to meet with her friends. Birgit flipped out over my painting. "This is so wonderful, Bernardo, I just knew you could do it! I suspected that you to have a talent for painting, but this is even better than I could have possibly imagined."

Jasi showed her the painting that she had made at school, as well as a new one she had started working on at home recently. You are very talented too, just like your father. You should keep developing that gift. And what kind of ring did you have in mind to make at my shop?" Jasi went to get a draft she had made.

"I would like a small plate with four little stones placed on top, with the plate being attached to the ring. The plate would be narrowly following the shape of my finger." Birgit looked very surprised.

"That's a brilliant idea! And why four stones?"

Jasi looked very thoughtful for a moment and then went on to explain, with shiny eyes: "One for mommy, one for me, and the other two for you and daddy." It was so touching. It appeared to be that the changes and difficult time we were experiencing in our lives made both my daughter and I more creative than ever before.

It was a couple weeks later when Anne told me she would like to move out of the house soon, and that she would start preparing to go and live with Mat. "Jasi can come over and stay with us any time she wants to," Anne said. The whole thing hit me like a hurricane, and a thousand thoughts were racing through my head once again.

"Now let's go slow with this, Anne. She hardly even knows Mat," I suggested.

Anne agreed, explaining that she had already been talking to Jasi about it, and that she'd prefer staying with me for now. I realized that for Anne this situation probably wasn't easy either, as I could imagine that she wanted to close her old life, and have a fresh start after falling in love with someone else. We had visited Mat a couple times in the past, and Jasi seemed to like him, which was something to build on. Nonetheless, I didn't want to rush things, preferring the course of events to develop and flow naturally.

"I've been thinking about this for a long time and it's what I want to do, and I'm prepared to deal with all the consequences. Mat and I really want to live together," she clarified.

I was fine with that, yet the thought of living alone with Jasi in this house was quite challenging, to say the least. It was going to be as much of a new life for me as the move away from home would be for Anne. After having had a companion and friend for the past 16 years, going to live on my own was a big change for me. I imagined that for Jasi things would be easier if she could continue to stay in her familiar environment.

I didn't sleep well that night, worrying about how all of this was going to play out. My next day at work wasn't much better, as I was hit with feelings of despair and anxiety. It was a downward spiral, which I wanted to stop as soon as possible. I decided to go down to *the rocks* after work, and I brightened up when I saw that Robbie was there. He must have sensed that I was going through something, and came over and sat down next to me.

"What's with you, Bernardo? You're not your usual self." I started explaining him my whole situation.

"I had noticed for a long time that things between you and Anne seemed difficult, and that she hadn't come with you to watch the sunset anymore, as she had done in the past. It seems she has changed," he said.

"She has. And I probably have changed too, but we haven't changed in the same direction. It's come to a point where I feel like I've been living with a stranger for the past years."

"Well, Bernardo, I can relate to that. My last relationship had ended up in a similar way. Katja wanted to go back to Germany to a more regular type of lifestyle. I could understand, as she didn't have good job opportunities here. One day, she was gone and so was the dog. All I found was a note on my bed. She said she was too scared to face me in person, as she didn't want to hurt me. I guess we just couldn't agree, with me wanting to stay here and her longing for a more regular life up in Germany."

He looked up over the sea, way into the distance. "I just couldn't imagine myself going back there and having to take on some job I wouldn't like. I enjoy it here; the pace of life is much slower than up north, and the climate and people here suit me. I prefer to live an alternative lifestyle, with no desire of going back to a boring life. It's easy for me to do my singing and windsurfing here."

"You're surfing?" I asked. "I hadn't heard about that." His eyes lit up.

"Of course I do, Bernardo. That's why I live out in El Medano, because the beach there is a windsurfer's paradise. Have you been there?" I had. It was a long sandy beach a few miles past the airport.

"I've been there several times with Jasi to fly our kites, which is great there because of the constant wind. We had noticed the many surfers, and had watched them do their fantastic jumps across the waves."

"Oh, you should try it Bernardo, I will teach you!"

"That sounds great! I would like to learn to do that. But first I need to pull through the whole situation with Anne. We have been communicating about it, and we even managed to muster up the courage to tell everything to our daughter. Yet the pain is immense," I explained.

"You guys are brave. It's not easy to face such a situation and try to solve it lovingly. When someone's feelings for you have changed, and they have the guts and honesty to tell you, it's hard, crushing, and devastating. Yet, it's so much better for them to be honest than to play a game with you, and for you to know the truth, and let them go. You clear the way for something that may be much better. It's hard at the beginning, but with time you will realize it was better this way. There is no use staying together when you're not pulling in the same direction."

I was glad for his encouragement, as he didn't preach, but spoke from personal experience.

Then, he suddenly changed topic: "I have my birthday in a couple of weeks, and I'm organising a party at my flat and at the beach. Will you come?"

"I'd love to! That's really sweet of you to invite me."

"Bernardo, join the club! Now we're both single. It's not that bad; I always find nice girls. I'm enjoying my time going solo right now."

As for me, I couldn't think too much about girls right now. I was more concerned about being a good father to Jasi, especially during this difficult time.

"Well, girls or rather young ladies, aren't off my mind completely, but right now I have other priorities."

"I understand. Just take it as it comes," he suggested.

The sun had set. It had gotten darker, but the peaceful splashing of the waves, and the good conversation, made it quite enjoyable to stay longer.

Robbie continued: "I'm glad that you and Anne decided to separate. I could see that you were no longer compatible. Anne seems to pursue a more materialistic lifestyle, while you're just a freak like me. I've seen her at parties where I have been invited to play music, and I felt quite bad for you. But I guess you're probably aware of all that."

"Well, maybe not totally, but I felt never really attracted to the kind of crowd she has gotten involved with. Some are just too snobby and materialistic for my taste. I'm just different. I enjoy sunsets, nature, good talks, music, and art. You know; things that don't require an expensive lifestyle that needs to be financed with endless hours at work. I enjoy being around people who are deep, but at the same time simple, like you and Birgit."

"We all change, for better or for worse. If people appear to change for worse we need to let them, because everyone has a right to find out for themselves where they will find fulfillment and where not. But I agree with you, I also prefer people who stay simple."

I was thinking about how Anne had changed. "Anne used to be like that too, very modest and satisfied with humble things, but through the years she just became so different." At this point I started crying as I felt a sadness coming over me, the great void in missing someone that is no longer there. "I miss the person she used to be. I didn't want to split up. I wanted to save Jasi from experiencing the heartache of it, and probably myself as well."

Robbie was putting his arm on my shoulder. "That's very understandable. But if Anne and you can both keep a peaceful and positive line of communication, then the new situation shouldn't be detrimental to any of you."

I slept better that night. The following day I called Robbie to tell him how much I had appreciated our talk the night before. "You're always welcome, Bernardo. I hope things continue to go well for you. Please feel free to call me anytime you feel like you need to talk," was his reply. I felt extremely thankful for this strong friendship.

Jasmine had taken up Birgit's offer to visit her shop, and sometime during the week she went there. "She is very sweet, she offered me to use four rounded turquoise stones for the ring. And later she even invited me for an ice-cream and we went to walk around Los Cristianos. We're continuing this week and are going to make the cast. I don't need to pay her anything, just something for the material needed for moulding. I'd like it to be silver. Will you pay for it?" she asked, looking at me with expecting eyes.

"Of course I will!" She was very excited about it. I think this new possibility helped spark her creativity, distracting her during this time when her mom was moving her own personal belongings away, little by little each day.

The next weekend I drove up to Puerto with Birgit, to bring some of her new creations, along with the cast of the ring they had designed. Jasi herself preferred spending the weekend with her friends. Tom had explicitly invited us to visit him at his house this time.

I was hoping to get a closer look at his garden. The Orotava valley has a lot of vegetation, resulting from the river flowing after rain, and it rains quite regularly on this northern part of the island. This kept the valley green and there were a lot of banana plantations, avocado trees, and lots of vegetables, whatever people had planted.

His house was quite a way up from Puerto, and was a touch bigger than mine, and with a lot more land around which hosted fruit, banana and avocado trees, and a large plot of vegetables.

Living on his own provided him with lots of time to work on the garden, and it looked very well kept. You could see that it was his pride and joy. He brought us around and showed us his plants, and they were gorgeous indeed: *Aloe Vera, Bougainvillea, Tajinaste, a gorgeous Echium Wildpretii*, various cacti, and, hidden away, a few cannabis plants.

"Now I know what you meant when you said you had some 'special plants' in your garden," I smiled. "Your garden is fantastic; it's a real paradise."

We sat down on his terrace, enjoying the fabulous view of the green valley rolling out into the blue Atlantic Ocean. Tom grilled some tomatoes, eggplant, and zucchini from his garden, which he then served with rice, *mojo*-sauce, and grilled pita bread. It was delicious. He accompanied the meal with some cold white wine, which he had bought from one of his neighbours.

"Everything grows here in the valley, whatever you plant. One just needs the time to take care of it, and I do have that time. And sometimes I just need to make time, which I did today, because at this hour I should be at my shop. But I don't want to live only to pay bills and then die," Tom said, kicking off the conversation.

"Bernardo has started to find his passion," Birgit chimed in.

"Oh, is that so? What is it?" he wanted to know.

"He has started painting, and his first painting is done. He has now begun work on a new one, but doesn't want to tell me what it is. It's a surprise for me, he says."

"Wow, I'd like to see that. I was thinking of buying a few paintings now that I've finished renovating my house. I've saved up some money for that, but I just haven't found the right paintings and painter yet. I'd like to have painting of some of my plants, the valley, Mount Teide, and the ocean in the back. That would match my house. Could you make one for me? I'd pay you for it. If I like it, I would get more as I need about ten of them, so I can spread them around. It's about the only thing missing now in my house." He paused for a minute. "And a wife, of course."

I was thrilled at this new possibility. Painting this lovely view from his garden was an attractive idea, and I made sure to take in as much of this wonderful view as possible, enabling me to recall and paint it later. I was pleased with the prospect of making some extra cash, as I was now paying off the credit for the house on my own.

It was a couple days before Robbie's birthday party that Anne had finalized her moving out. The parents of Jasi's friend had invited her to go with them for a long weekend to the island of El Hierro, where they owned a little house. She was very excited to go with them, as she had never been there. "I will take paper and paint along, so I can make a painting for you of the view there."

I was glad she could go away for a few days. Anne's moving out was not easy for us, neither did it seem so for Anne, but we didn't talk about that. I spent the next night alone at our house and it felt quite strange. I had started the painting which I wanted to give to Birgit. I had made sketches of a woman sitting on the rocks, putting seashells on a string. It reminded me of her and I missed her. We had been getting very close lately, and I felt very safe around her. My thoughts and secrets were in good hands. Too bad she didn't feel like getting emotionally close to anyone, or at least not to me.

I was now officially single, but I felt like I had been single for a long time, and was longing for some loving arms around me, some sweet kisses, and passion. I hadn't felt Birgit was ready for that, but I was very thankful for her and Robbie's friendship at a time when I suddenly found myself alone with my life.

Chapter 7: Sun and fun

I found the ride out to Robbie's place very interesting; especially the last part. One follows a small road that turns off from the highway, leading down to this old fishing village by the ocean. There are no curves, but just a long straight road through this desert-like countryside. I noticed occasional plastic-covered banana plantations on both sides. I'd been told that bananas only grow within some wind protection, and this area of the island is indeed very windy. That is what brings a lot of windsurfers to this place. El Medano is a somewhat of a sleepy little place out in nowhere, and the reflection of the sun on the small white buildings comes as a nice contrast to Los Cristianos with its large apartment complexes.

The sun was beating down strongly, and at this hour the streets were quite deserted. Only the restaurants down at the beachfront had their terraces filled with tourists having lunch in the shade. However, most of the people were out in the ocean with their surfboards, enjoying the strong breeze this place offered.

I found Robbie's apartment easily, as it was above one of the cafeterias. The owner who rented it out to Robbie also managed the cafeteria. The flat was on the top floor, and had a large wind-protected sun terrace, from where one could see the sea. I gave Robbie the painting I'd made for him.

"Oh, this is marvellous! And what amazing colours! It looks rather psychedelic; I get high just looking at it. You painted it just like I'd experienced it as well, giving it your own touch. It's amazing!" I was glad that he liked it, and to receive some encouragement.

He showed it to the two young ladies who had already

arrived, and he introduced us to each other. Anouk and Betje were both from Holland. "I'd met them while out singing. They went for two weeks to La Gomera, and now they've just come back and will be staying here for another week. I'm teaching them to surf". He seemed all excited, and I didn't blame him; they both looked very sweet. I told them about my various visits to Amsterdam during my hippie days.

"Please tell us more about it, Bernardo! We were born a handful of years too late and just missed it," Anouk said excitedly.

We got into a very lively conversation while Robbie served us some vegetarian paella he had made, accompanied by some freshly made sangria. We all commented on his food, and how delicious it was. It turned out that the girls had rented an apartment nearby, but Anouk had apparently already sort of moved in with Robbie. They seemed to get along great, and were all over each other. Robbie had given them their first windsurfing lesson that morning.

"The conditions were incredible this morning, Bernardo, you should come along next time," Betje suggested.

Anouk agreed: "We're just learning the basics now, but it's a lot of fun, and Robbie is a good teacher. After our lesson, we were watching him as he was speeding around out at sea, and he had such a great time. I hope one day I'll be able to do this as fast as he does."

"He has already offered to teach me some lessons. I just need to find the time," I replied. I was glad for Robbie having found something he was enjoying so much.

"We already know quite a lot about Robbie and his exciting lifestyle. Would you care to tell us a about yours?" I had three pair of eyes looking expectantly at me.

"Why are you looking at me too, Robbie? You already know it." He smiled. "It's an exciting story, Bernardo. I'd love to hear it again."

I started telling them my life-story in a nutshell, about how Anne and I had travelled around, and how we ended up having our lovely daughter, and settling down here in Tenerife. They were listening very intently, and seemed especially interested in the way we handled our separation and our daughter's care.

"It is more very difficult to live as a hippie on your own, when there's no more movement," Betje said. "I became a hippie too, even though by that time the era was over. Even in Amsterdam I noticed less and less travellers, and somehow the movement had vanished. No one seems to know how and where to, just as the saying goes: 'Where have all the hippies gone?' Nonetheless, I wanted to be one no matter what, because I liked the ideology, and so I've been one ever since."

"Well," I said, "The hippie days were both tragic and happy: It was a tragedy that we couldn't succeed with our ideas for a better world. But we were glad to find many cool people who gathered around spirituality, good music, the sunset, and a blade of grass."

"I especially like the blade of grass," Robbie said with a smile.

I went on: "Regarding your question as to 'Where have all the hippies gone', I have the following theory: While some continued their lifestyle in a still and quiet manner; many got disillusioned because they couldn't change the world; others started having kids and had to make a living; and the rest probably became everything that they had been against."

"That sounds like a plausible explanation, Bernardo. You're probably right," Betje said somewhat sadly. "But one can still be a hippie today; you just need the right ingredients: Peace, love, understanding, tolerance, simplicity, and a desire to be and act differently than all the rest."

Someone rang at the door, which put an end to the conversation. It was Birgit, passing by to give her birthday greetings to Robbie. She gave him a fabulous hemp necklace with a fluorite stone in it. She was on her way up to Tom with some new creations that she wanted to get moulded. I was sad she couldn't stay. She gave me a long hug, and it felt so good. For the first time, I felt like I missed her being close to me.

"Sorry I can't stay. I have a few timely orders that need to get finished. Have a nice time!" she said as she went on her way. *She's seeing Tom quite a lot,* went through my mind. But what else could I do with such disturbing thoughts, other than chasing them away and tune in to myself and what I was doing right now.

We all moved to the terrace, where the girls took off their clothes to sunbathe. I sat down next to Betje, and she asked me to put some sunscreen lotion on her back, which of course, I didn't mind doing at all.

"I did my social studies in Amsterdam, and now I'm helping out at a youth centre for teenagers in difficult situations, trying to help them find their way in life," she explained.

"That's a very worthy cause."

"Yes, I'm quite passionate about it, and I can see how some lives change right in front of my eyes, but it takes time. And judging by your fantastic painting, it looks like you have found your passion too."

"Yes, and I'm very excited about it. This painting is the first one I made, and I can't describe the feeling I had while creating it. I can't get home fast enough these days to continue."

"I love the arts," she said. "I've visited the van Gogh exhibition in Amsterdam several times already. Have you seen it?"

"Yes, I have. My favourite paintings are the ones with cypress trees. I call it 'The Tree of the South', as I connect them to summer and crickets; freedom and travelling; spending the nights in my sleeping bag somewhere under a starry sky, while hitch-hiking towards warmer climates," I explained.

"That sounds awesome."

"Sleeping under a starry sky always made me feel at ease, and left my mind undisturbed by human noise. And even though there were thousands of crickets singing their song, I considered them to be a part of the silence. Noise, for me, started only at the point where it was made by humans. And, I don't know why Vincent's paintings remind me so much of those travelling days. Sometimes we make connections to things and can't even fully understand why."

"I know what you mean. I think his paintings connect a lot of people to that kind of magic, that's why he's so popular. It's a similar feeling you get when passing by certain shops with all the different smells emerging out on the street, reminding you of something that has happened somewhere in time. Just like with pictures or paintings, it seems that smells stay registered in our minds as well, connecting us to certain events. Music can have that kind of effect too. Our senses of perception are a lot more important than we assume. At the same time, we know so little about them, as the main emphasis at school is on feeding the brain."

"If you love the arts, do you do something creative on the side?" I wanted to know.

"I keep a diary and sometimes I write poems," she answered. "But I haven't let anyone read them."

"Oh, I'd love to read them, you should send them to me."

"I might just do that," she smiled.

I continued: "The fact that there are still creative people left on this planet needs to be celebrated. Too many people just don't think they could be creative. But even raising a peppermint plant on their balcony could be considered as being creative, making it possible for nature to grow."

"That's so true Bernardo. Helping nature to recreate itself is a wonderful piece of art. I always enjoy gardening and would often help my dad when visiting my parents at their village."

"Thinking about it, art is a very wonderful thing, because it helps us express how we feel about the things we see, and the effect they're having on us. I believe art has to be felt by our senses, much more so than being interpreted by our brain," I added.

"I think so too. I read somewhere that the arts won't change the world. I can't believe that! If nothing else, art might help preserve nature's beauty in the minds of the viewers, the wonder and the mystical energy it leaves us with. Because I believe nature itself is the greatest art, and its perception by painters connects the viewer to such beauty. Since there is general destruction of such splendour happening all around us, art itself is very much needed to help preserve natures' value and magic, serving as a constant reminder of it."

"Yes, that's why I like the impressionists, because they didn't just paint nature as it seemed to their eyes, but interpreting into their paintings the magical effect it had on them. Later in history, some art became more abstract, but I find that interesting too, as it gets one to think. So, I believe, art doesn't need to exclude the brain, one just needs to know when to use it and when not."

"Art shouldn't have to be explained. It's the same with our life. We shouldn't need to have to explain it to people. In that sense our life can become a piece of art as well," she expressed.

"Yes," I agreed. "Either people will like it or they won't."

"Did you travel a lot, Bernardo?"

"I did so in my younger years, travelling and hitchhiking throughout Europe, before settling down on the island here."

"I guess for us girls it was never so safe to try to catch a ride, and nowadays people hardly do it anymore, as criminality has increased."

"Yes, the world is definitely not becoming a safer place. It has gotten to be riskier than in the 70ties, when we had no worries, and I used to even hitchhike alone. Nowadays, I would prefer going around in a camper."

"It's nice to get to know you, Bernardo. I think you would be a nice person to travel with."

"Well, I do enjoy travelling, but haven't done much in recent years. We went a few times to visit our parents in Switzerland, but apart from that we've stayed mainly on the island," I sighed nostalgically.

"I should travel more too, as you did. School and university do very little besides preparing you for making money, and becoming part of a very materialistic society. If you want to know what life is all about, you need to travel and get in touch with other, more simple ways to live. And, you may find the perfect place to stay and support yourself, even though the whole world around you may totally disapprove of it."

"I see it like that too, Betje. We can choose not to be a part of that rat-race, chasing money and career to afford a materialistic lifestyle. There are ways to live modestly, with fewer bills, resulting in a more peaceful and stress-free life. With more time for travelling, for spending time out in nature or for doing something creative."

"I'd love to travel in a camper throughout all of Europe; that would be fun. But with the right partner, not just with anybody."

"You don't have a boyfriend?" I wondered.

"I've had a few, but nothing serious. It's hard to find the right person. And, in the beginning, you never know which turns a relationship will take, or if it would even last longer than the initial being in love phase."

"True. But you can't always let love slip by, just because of fear that it might not work out. What if it would?"

"Yes, but at the same time, one doesn't really enjoy getting hurt right and left. I've learned to drop my expectations in that sense, and that has helped me. I do enjoy romance and sex, but I have learned not to expect it to turn into a steady relationship. I've been less hurt that way, as if you don't expect too much, you won't be disappointed. At least I haven't turned into a love-starved and sexually frustrated freak," she retorted.

"Well, I guess that description might better fit me lately. But I've been keeping myself busy with other things."

"That's ok too. And, you have a daughter to care for and a new passion to keep you busy. But don't let all of life pass you by, there is some fun out there to be had," she said with a twinkle in her eye.

"I used to get fed up with guys who would fall in love with me, awakening hopes for something more serious, and then leave me after the initial spark had gone. But then I realized that I didn't particularly like some guys either after getting to know them better. And in that case, I would be the one to leave them. We just can't always blame others for things we do ourselves as well. After all, if I find out that I don't match with someone, why should I continue to stay with them just for the sake of not hurting them? But anway, all these implications haven't stopped me from enjoying romance and sex. I need it," she admitted.

"Yes, so do I."

"Hey, you guys, let's go to the beach! I'm expecting quite a few people to appear," Robbie stated excitedly.

He was ready with his guitar, asking us to help carry some other stuff along. We then headed down all along the beach towards the far end of it, to the more secluded part where tourists and surfers wouldn't usually go.

"The sun will set in a couple of hours. One of my friends and I brought some wood here yesterday so that we can make a fire tonight."

It seemed like Robbie was well prepared for this. Some of his friends were already there with drums and another guitar. The girls began taking off their clothes and jumping into the water for a swim.

"Come on Bernardo," Betje called, signalling me to go in as well.

I jumped in after her, and everyone else joined in as well. The girls splashing water at us, and us pushing them under water, contributed to a lot of fun. Betje snuck up on me from behind and gave me a hug. It had been a long time since I had felt someone that close, and it felt extremely good. Later we found ourselves laying on the sand, letting our skin dry in the warm sun.

It's amazing what a calming feeling I always get when listening to the waves, I thought to myself.

"I love the sea. When I sit at the ocean, it's like each wave washes one more sorrow away, endlessly. In the end, there is nothing left to worry about. That's what nature does to me," I expressed.

"That's why I love riding those waves, Bernardo. They wash away my sadness," Robbie joined in. He then began kissing Anouk.

Oh boy! That would wash my sadness away too, I contemplated. Betje was looking at me and seemed to be studying my face. I noticed that her eyes were brown, like mine.

Robbie and some of his friends had started to play music, and it created a lovely atmosphere. More people had shown up in the meantime as we all greeted each other. They were playing very inspired music, and Robbie was obviously enjoying his birthday, with Anouk snuggling up to him. I was just thinking how nice it would be to have someone doing the same to me, when I felt Betje's head on my shoulder.

"Come, I'd like to walk along the beach, it's so amazing tonight." She pulled me up in the direction she wanted to take me. "I know a hidden place nearby. I was there sunbathing with Anouk a couple days ago."

We walked along the beach, still hearing the distant sound of the drums and guitars. She pulled me towards the water.

"It's chilly at this hour with the sun setting," I protested, but she was just laughing. As she fell into the water, she pulled me in along with her. It wasn't as cold as I had imagined, especially as I felt her warm body against mine.

"Are you not used to a woman snuggling up to you, Bernardo?"

"Probably not," I laughed.

"I like you Bernardo, you're so real."

Then she kissed me with her salty lips and it felt amazing. It was high time for me to loosen up and enjoy the moment. As we laid down on the sand, I tasted the salt on her skin as I started kissing her all over. She seemed to enjoy it, and was clinging to me like she hadn't had such attention for quite some time as well. The nearby waves came crashing, and dampened the sounds that we made as we loved each other in a wild session of sand, salt, and passion.

"You are so sweet, Bernardo, and such a good lover," she whispered in my ear.

I was wondering how long it had been since I had heard something like that. We loved each other several times and forgot the world around us; and yes, we even forgot the sea, the moon, and the stars. Until we finally lay down exhausted, watching some stars shooting across the sky.

"Did you wish something, Bernardo?"

"Well," I answered. "When I wish something, I usually pray. However, right now I wished that all the people who don't have it as good as us would be comforted."

"That's such a sweet thought, Bernardo. I thanked God for this wonderful experience with you, and I just wished that everything would go well with my future once I arrive back in Holland."

"I hope that for you as well," I affirmed. She invited me to spend the night at her place, and I gladly accepted.

The next day we all met for breakfast at Robbie's place, after stopping by the bakery for some fresh bread. "Bernardo, you guys suddenly disappeared, what happened?" Robbie asked with a big smile. "We went for a walk and got lost." Now Anouk was laughing too. "The same thing happened to Robbie and I the other night. It's a very romantic place," she said knowingly.

I had an excellent weekend, and when I left, I was in very high spirits. Betje and I met up a couple more times before they needed to return to Holland. We harmonized well, but it didn't seem like we got as far as wanting to start some serious relationship.

The evening after the girls had left I went down to *the rocks* when work was done. Birgit was there, and she seemed quite down, while I was still quite upbeat after the lovely time I'd had.

"What is it?" I tried to find out. "I have been confused about my feelings, Bernardo. I am outright scared to have someone love me. What if their feelings might be the same as mine, but then change? You know how scary that is?"

It is indeed, if you think about it. A lot of things in life can be scary, but then again, life is more about living than thinking.

"And you know how difficult it is to even understand my feelings in the first place? How much love does one need to feel for someone to know whether it's real or not, and whether you should go to bed with them or not?" she added.

"Those are questions that do arise in life, that's true. I guess you speak from some hurtful experiences you've had, and you obviously don't want to get hurt again, nor end up hurting someone else. Unfortunately, there is just no way to go through life without ever hurting anybody, or ever getting hurt, unless you'd stop interacting with anyone closely. However, that might bring on problems with solitude. As soon as you get close to people, shit happens, and needs to be taken care of."

"That's exactly right, Bernardo. The minute I will give my heart to someone, they will have the power to hurt me immensely. Maybe I belonged to the more conservative fraction of hippies; I was never into this *free love* thing. Were you?" She looked at me, awaiting my reply.

"Ha! What a question! I guess I was a bit of everything. I do understand people who want to have sex while they are waiting for the perfect partner to come around, if that might ever even happen. Someone who would never ever hurt them, if such a person even exists. I mean, who would want to go through life without sex and romance, just waiting for Mr or Mrs Perfect to come along some distant day?"

"Yes, that's why I am scared right now to fall in love again. Though I would actually like to and would need it."

"But you can get hurt in a relationship even through daily routine," I carried on. "The perception of hurt seems to be a very individual one. If we get hurt by every little thing, a relationship can turn into hell too. But it could also turn into heaven and you will never know if you never try."

She was quiet, and it seemed like she was deep in thought about what I'd just said.

"But, to answer your question more specifically regarding *free love*: I do believe in the personal freedom of two consenting partners to have sex, knowing that their time of passion and love may be just for a moment, and not meant to be forever. I call that freedom. And yes, I do allow myself such pleasure occasionally, if it ever happens."

"You do, Bernardo?" She looked at me somewhat bewildered. "I have never been into this. I was always looking for the right person to start a relationship first, before getting into having sex. I guess we must be quite different in that sense."

"Well, then let's at least celebrate the differences," I suggested. She smiled and pulled out a joint.

"Let's celebrate."

The sun was setting in all its glory. How amazing that each sunset is a new show, and totally different from all previous ones. No sunset is the same. Each time it sets up different scenarios in collaboration with the clouds, the sea, and the sky. It's unpredictable.

"Every sunset is unique. It's not so bad to be unpredictable, Birgit. It's a type of opposite to being boring. Sometimes we need to take ourselves by surprise, and do some daring, cool and good shit that will make us be amazed at ourselves."

"Bernardo, I've always liked you; since we first met. But, because of your situation and the problems with your family, I resisted getting emotionally involved with you. I've shied away from this situation," she explained. "And then recently, Tom and I started a romantic episode. That's why I didn't come to Robbie's party, I wanted to go and be with him. In a way, everything made sense: We share the same passion, could use our synergies to develop both of our shops, and eventually be moving together to start a family."

I was quietly listening to these latest developments. *Her and Tom*, I thought, and didn't know if I should feel jealous. I probably did, even though I knew I had no right to feel like that.

"But after the initial romance, I am not sure about my feelings for him," she continued. "I'd like to get out of this again, preferably without hurting him. But I have no clue as to how I should go about doing that. I'm extremely confused right now, and in need of getting myself together. What do you think I should do?"

That was not such an easy situation she'd gotten herself into. But at least she had tried to get close to someone again, I

73

realized.

"I think you should listen to your heart. For sure it's crappy that someone might get hurt if you started something and now want to hop off, but you will eventually need to be honest about your feelings." I didn't know what else to say, as this was a time for her to examine her own heart and react accordingly.

I felt sorry for her, as it's not a pleasant situation to find yourself in. "You're right, Bernardo, I will need to follow my heart. Once I will be sure about my feelings, I'm going to tell him. Pray for me," she asked. "I need it."

Chapter 8: Whisked away

Time passed quickly since I had gotten into painting. It was on one such night as I was busy with the first piece I was working on for Tom, that the phone rang. It was Robbie: "Bernardo, it's so good to hear you!" I just loved that excitement in his voice, as I could be sure he had something new up his sleeve.

After filling each other in on the latest news, he asked me if I wanted to go with him and two young ladies up Mount Teide for the weekend, as there would be a full moon that night, and that would be "trippy", as he called it. It sounded exciting, and we agreed that I'd be going to his place and we'd drive up to Las Canadas from there.

I would have liked for Birgit to come along as well, but when asking her about it, she said she had a timely project that needed to be finished, some major order someone had placed. She explained that for the next two weeks she would be very busy, including having to go up to see Tom a couple of times to ensure her creations would turn out the way she needed them.

Tom, I thought. I very much liked him, but I felt a breeze of jealousy touching my heart again, brought on by the thought of them spending so much time together. It was probably all based on insecurity, but since I wasn't even sure of my own feelings for her it seemed better not to take such thoughts too far. Instead, I was sending out a little prayer for them as I knew from our last conversation that they were going through some rough times regarding the future of their relationship.

Since we were going to spend the night on the top of a high mountain, I took a warm sweater and jacket along, as it can get cold at night, even during the summer. During the winter months, it would sometimes snow so much up there that the local government had to close the roads, and even forbid all hikers from going up there. I took my sleeping bag, a flashlight and a few other provisions, including some food, and put them all into my backpack.

At Robbie's I met Sue and Melanie, two friends of his visiting from Denmark. Of course, Robbie was giving them surf lessons. They were lovely. I took note that Robbie had a fine taste when it came to ladies. I liked the kind that didn't necessarily look beautiful to society's standards, but with a natural flair about them. Having an open mind, ready for discussions about God and the world, without wanting to escape taking a position, nor being set in boxed-in ideas. I always enjoyed talking to people who had their own opinion, even if wasn't always the same as mine.

We drove up the mountain and got on the gondola in the late afternoon. The ride was, as I already knew, quite short, but when getting out of the cabin we noticed that the temperature had dropped considerably, even though the sun was still up.

Before leaving I had called Jasi to tell her that I wouldn't be home for the weekend, as I'd be going up to Mount Teide. She appreciated that I informed her of my plans and absence, yet added: "But please take good care of yourself; I don't want anything bad to happen to you. Promised?"

"Of course, my girl," I reassured her. "I don't believe in bad things happening. If something so-called bad were to happen, I think it would turn out to be something I need; teaching me some needed life-lessons."

She still seemed to be worried, and I couldn't understand why. I knew she was very sensitive to spiritual matters, which made me wonder why she would feel that way. However, I wasn't going to let that take away my joy of going to watch the full moon with my friends. As always, I wasn't planning on doing some risky rock-climbing or whatever else might possibly lead up to accidents, as that wasn't part of my nature. Of course, accidents could always happen, even when trying our best to prevent them from doing so.

"Don't worry, baby. You know I don't do dangerous stuff. And, it's less dangerous being out in nature than it is being downtown nowadays. Out in the wild, where nature is in control, you don't need to fear anything. Down in the cities, where humanity is in control, you need to fear almost everything. I'm just going to have some fun with my friends. We'll be watching the full moon from up there, it will be amazing. I'll call you on Monday and tell you all about it."

"I often get these feelings, like something would be about to happen, and then it does. I can't even tell if it's going to be something good or bad, and that worries me," she explained hesitantly.

She had told me before about some *déjà-vu* experiences she'd had. But even more often she would have feelings, or premonitions, that something important was going to happen, but she couldn't determine if it would turn out for good or bad.

"I know we've already talked about this, and I still believe the same way as I explained to you last time. When you consider all the things happening to us from day to day, the actual sum of bad things happening is extremely low, as most of the things we experience are positive. Unless of course we put ourselves continuously into harm's way, or hang around negative people and situations," I reminded her.

"Yes, I thought about that, and I came to the same conclusion. And I've recently started distancing myself from certain friends that didn't seem to have a good influence on me. I became aware that we need to watch out about who and what takes away our inner peace and quietness, swaying us into becoming something we are not. Then we need to work slowly, or fast if possible, on removing those things and people from our lives. It's a difficult road to take, but necessary to preserve our sanity."

"That's very smart thinking."

"I've started writing down stuff like that in my diary, and it's helped me in being able to refer back to these written thoughts when getting confused in certain situations. I've written so much stuff down during the past year, I could probably start writing a book."

"Maybe you should, Jasi. The world certainly needs more spiritual input." She seemed to calm down.

"Take care, Daddy. And remember, I will always love you."

I was thinking over that last conversation with my daughter while we were forging ahead and up the last stretch, from the gondola station to the peak. There was a little wind facing us, not exactly warm, but not unpleasant either. Upon arriving, Robbie set up a little battery operated loudspeaker along with his Walkman, enabling us to start listening to some nice sounds while talking and waiting for the sun to set. It was thrilling to be so high up; like being on top of the world. In moments like these, I would almost forget that the world was controlled by humanity. It made me and my problems feel so insignificant in comparison to nature and the universe, and mankind so ridiculous in trying to control things.

"Robbie, look how nature and the universe is in control. No one can stop the show!" It just burst out of me.

"You're right Bernardo. Yet, mankind is dealing out a lot of damage upon the ecosystem. There is no escape valve for all the bad air we're producing each day. It all accumulates within the hemisphere. And who breathes in that stuff eventually? We all do, and so do the animals and plants."

Sue started adding her part to the conversation: "That's right. It's evident that those of us growing up in all these manmade cities have a harder time remembering where we all come from, and are more likely to lose touch with nature and our own souls. The best medicine is to get out of those man-made cities and out to nature, to the mountains, or the ocean."

She seemed to be quite taken by this topic. "Don't you all feel tired sometimes of being part of a species that is so cruel to each other, and to other living beings?"

"I surely do so, Sue." I replied, "The world's indeed a *fucked-up* place. But, if you go out into nature, to where mankind hasn't brought chaos yet, you will find the most splendid, pure energy, light, and peace. That's the only purity you can find these days, as everything else is polluted by mankind's greed, confusion and industrialization."

She continued: "I'm not religious. And whether you believe in a creator or not, you can't help but admit that nature is so incredibly perfect and overflowing with the warmest and purest energy. Mankind would do good in honouring, preserving, and living in harmony with the environment, as with each other."

I pondered all that was being said, while staring upwards. I noticed the first star had appeared in the darkening sky. *It's been said the first one to appear is Venus,* I thought.

"Sometimes I wish I could just take off to the stars; that some aliens would come and take me on a trip to see a better world than this one. Even if just for a few hours, or days, or maybe weeks. It would be so refreshing."

"I don't know if I'd like to depart with aliens, Bernardo. I'd be scared to be somewhere out of this world, not even considering the concerns about whether aliens would come with good intentions or not," Sue said. She seemed to be unsure about what kind of aliens to expect, so I decided to take their side.

"If aliens were to come for a visit to Earth, I think they'd come with good intentions. I don't think they'd be delighted to visit all the slaughterhouses, or watch what's happening in the warzones, or see poor people getting exploited. I assume that if aliens existed, they would be good creatures; better than humans."

"Why do you think so?" Sue inquired.

"Because, I tend to think that being worse than mankind is nearly impossible."

"That's so true," Melanie said thoughtfully. "But I'd be sort of scared of them too, I guess due to fear of the unknown. Perhaps all that I see and feel provides me with a certain feeling of security."

"It's nice to hear your opinion on this, Melanie."

"It's been said that the quieter ones are the more

dangerous ones, because they think thoughts no one knows about," she mentioned with a shy sort of smile.

"You are a smart woman. You almost make me feel bad for talking so much," I smiled back.

"Well, Bernardo, would you want to know what I really think?" she continued.

"Of course! You know, I can also listen, not just talk. Tell us, please."

"I think we're quite often visited by aliens. Many people report having seen them. But I don't trust those pictures shown of UFO's. My suggestion is that when they come, they do so by surprise and unexpectedly. That's why so few people have enough time to pull out their cameras. Maybe they are rather shy creatures, like me."

Robbie joined in: "I don't think we should need to be afraid of them. I'm probably more scared of some evil humans. I believe that if we are curious, and go to explore nature and the world around us, we will be less afraid of aliens, or death, or whatever. That is because we will have gotten used to being interested and curious, and looking forward to new things and situations."

He started eating a sandwich, so we all pulled out the various snacks we had brought along.

"Robbie has a good point," I agreed. "And, in being more interested in spiritual things rather than materialism, any fear of death is greatly reduced. He who is not greatly attached to this world will have an easier time to let it go."

"I guess in that sense, Melanie and I aren't as adventurous as you guys seem to be. But I would like to grow spiritually, for one thing. Being adventurous is all right, but I think being spiritually interested is also very important," Sue added. "I'm sure we all realize that there are different levels of awakening. If someone even just realizes that materialism doesn't lead to spirituality, they will already be greatly enlightened. And once they realize that we are all one, that's certainly another level, and so on. It's basically up to us as to how far we decide to go with love and light."

"Sue is right. Maybe the limits to spiritual growth are only in our minds and hearts." Melanie was now fully entering the conversation. "Spiritual awakening can either be a process, or a sudden realization that our spiritual growth is so much more important than the materialistic world around us, and it gets us to start searching. You won't need expensive hours of yoga and meditation courses, or enlightenment seminars to find spirituality. It can't be bought, it's free. If it could be paid for, even the rich would find it."

"Very true," Sue continued. "That's an amazing thing about spiritual enlightenment. Some people can go on with their life for years, and then suddenly something happens to them, and they start being interested in spiritual things."

"You girls are very smart. That's why I am so glad you decided to come up the mountain with us," Robbie said, with a touch of admiration in his voice.

We were quiet for a minute. We could already see the shape of the moon. The sun was still shining, but I suddenly got this weird feeling. Nothing negative though, but rather a sudden premonition at that moment, with the sunlight diminishing and the moon coming up. *Maybe there is some connection to what Jasi had mentioned*, I thought.

"Well, perhaps we were put here to grow spiritually. Not too many people seem to realize that, and they get into this materialistic trip, trying to build themselves an eternal home here on Earth, forgetting all about looking up at the stars. We mustn't keep our eyes on all the horror that's going on in the world; otherwise we'll get depressed, just like so many people do. We can't close our eyes to all the pain and suffering either, but it should be balanced out by keeping our eyes on all the beauty that still surrounds us."

"That's right on, Bernardo. If we all would just enhance ourselves spiritually we could start enjoying this paradise we were put in, and treat it and all living beings with utter respect." We were all in silence for a moment, thinking about Robbie's words.

He was very spiritual, my friend Robbie, once you got to

know him better. At first glance he seemed just like some easy-going guy who enjoys surfing, music, weed, and girls, in whatever order. But there was a lot more depth to him once you got to know him. He appeared in many ways more outgoing than me, and I appreciated that in him. I noticed how much I loved him, and how close we had gotten over the past year. We had watched so many sunsets together, had so many highly interesting and positive discussions, as well as just a lot of plain fun together. We knew each other well by now, and could always talk about deep things. It seemed that either one of us could think, say or do anything, and there would be no judgement from the other.

"Well, it's time to enhance ourselves even more." He pulled out a joint and started lighting it. It was right on time, as the sun slowly began to set.

"I'll see you on the dark side of the moon," escaped softly from the small loud-speakers.

"That's the right song for this scenery, Robbie," Sue said. "Indeed. I wonder if they had spent a night watching the full moon before writing that album. Anyway, I always felt there was something special about the moon. Think about the harmonious relationship the sun and the moon have, without ever touching each other. When one goes down on the horizon, the other one starts shining, a little less brightly, but just as important to guide *lonely travellers* at night."

"People have given the moon a lot of significance throughout history," Robbie continued. "I don't want to spiritualize everything, but one thing is for sure: the moon and the sun go somewhat hand in hand in preserving us from total darkness. Maybe the moon is to represent hope, for if you have hope, you can still see in the dark."

"Robbie, you should have become a priest, you sound so comforting," Melanie commented. We all had a good laugh.

"Being a priest is not such a bad job. You comfort people going through stuff, and remind those at the grave that they too must go one day. Otherwise, they might prefer to never give any thought to that. But just as we think about life, we should also sometimes do so about death. We live more fully that way, I think."

"That's true, but where do we go when we depart from this world?" Sue seemed to be very interested in that question. It was certainly an interesting topic for all of us. I don't know how many hours we had asked ourselves such questions at past sunsets, or situations leading to long hours of philosophy and speculation.

"Bernardo and I suspect that some things will remain a mystery probably right up to the moment when we depart from this world. And who knows how much more we'll actually get to know when we die?"

We had passed a couple joints around, and it started taking effect. "Where's that herb from? It seems to be from a good garden," I asked Robbie.

"It's from Juan; he has a few plants growing somewhere. It's the same stuff we had last time."

"Well, this herb sure gets one thinking," I said, as we watched the big red sun dive down into the sea, leaving a long trail of shimmering light across the Atlantic Ocean.

Robbie turned off the music, and it was suddenly very quiet. Some other groups of people hanging out not far from us had been rather loud before. Someone had even brought a guitar with them, but they had stopped playing in the meantime. There now was an eerie silence in the air. With the sun gone, it had gotten darker, but the moon was so bright today that it was difficult to see the stars, as the moon was outshining them all.

"It's so quiet up here when no one talks," Sue interrupted the silence. "It seems like the whole world has stopped." The girls leaned their heads on our shoulders, and we snuggled up. We did this in part because it was getting quite chilly, but perhaps also because of the magic of this moment. Sue continued: "The moon is shining brighter than usual. Or maybe that's just because we're watching it from up here."

Robbie unrolled his sleeping bag, as it had gotten chilly, and we all followed suit. Melanie cuddled up to me.

"I could die like this, Bernardo," Robbie said. "Ha, so could I; but I don't think we'll die like this."

We were quiet again. Sometimes you just don't know what to say anymore, and silence is something to be highly treasured. And there are times, like now, when silence would impose itself and demand speechlessness.

"Doesn't the moon seem brighter than just ten minutes ago?" Sue was wondering.

"True, I noticed that too," Robbie answered as she curled up closer to him.

"It's only in such silence that we can feel the real power of the universe. It would do people a lot of good to spend time in silence. The world would be different if people were to do that," Melanie said, as she huddled even closer to me.

"Look, guys, the moon is getting even brighter!" Robbie sat up.

"That's amazing. I have never seen such a bright full moon either." We all sat up, so we could have a better view. We looked at each other and could see each other's faces as if it were in broad daylight.

"What's this, Bernardo? Holy shit!" Robbie looked at me with a mixed look of shock and astonishment.

"I don't know Robbie. I have never seen such a thing before. This is amazing!"

"Look, guys, I see some lights dancing around the moon!" Sue must have had very sharp eyes; I couldn't see that. I noticed Melanie clinging to me, like she would be scared.

"Don't be afraid guys. This is just another spectacle of nature which is to be enjoyed. It doesn't matter if the world's scientists didn't warn us of this. It's wonderful!" I tried to calm her down.

"Now I can see those lights too, Bernardo, Sue was right!" Robbie said excitedly.

By now we had all gotten up, hoping that we'd be able to see them as well. Finally, I detected a few small lights circling around the moon. The problem was that the moon was so bright it hurt my eyes to look directly into it. Melanie was no longer the silent girl she had been at the beginning of the evening.

"Wow, there are more and more lights around the moon. I can't count them anymore." Now I could see them better. It looked like the moon was spitting them out, like sparks from a volcano, and there were more and more of them.

"This is fascinating. I never thought I'd witness such a thing in my life, and I feel very positive and peaceful vibes coming from all this. This rocks, let's enjoy it!" I said, as I threw my arms up into the sky.

"Look! Some of the lights are moving away from the moon and going out into space." Sue, with her sharp eyes, was like a soldier on the watchtower of a castle, letting everyone inside know what was happening.

I wondered if Jasi would also be able to observe this from Madrid. It's so much more difficult to see such things from within a city, because of all the light pollution there. I think we were extremely blessed to be up here tonight, where we could observe the moon so closely, although by now it was turning into something that appeared to be much more than a regular full moon. I missed Jasi. *God, be with her*, I prayed.

I could now also distinguish some lights dispersing away from the moon, and I was wondering where they'd go.

"There are hundreds of them!" Sue screamed. It wasn't a scream of fear, but more like one of great wonder.

I guess all of us here had some spiritual experiences of some sort in the past, or at least believed in them, or thought they were possible. Maybe that explains why noone among us seemed to be experiencing real fear or panic.

"This is impressive, Bernardo. And it's not only because of that little weed we smoked, this is really happening!"

"Ah, Robbie, maybe this is just some very good stuff that Juan produced in his garden," I joked. But of course, it was too late for jokes, because our *watchtower*, Sue, was now announcing that they had formed into large groups and were "staring at the world", as she put it.

"Wow, I hope they have good intentions, Bernardo."

Now, for the first time, I noticed a touch of anxiety in Robbie's voice.

"Robbie, why should the universe let us down now, after allowing us to be born into this world? Or, if they might come to harm, maybe they might harm all those industrialists who keep damaging Mother Earth. We are gentle as lambs, who would want to harm us?" We laughed our fears away.

I don't know why I had so much peace. Maybe it was because of that magnificent experience I'd had in my youth, when I had prayed and cried out to the universe to take that spirit of fear from me while getting onto a bad trip, resulting from too much of some drug. There I had found such incredible peace, and had become one with the surrounding energy of the plants and trees.

The girls were now keeping quiet, just holding on to us. I don't know why in times like these our shoulders were suddenly something very valuable.

"They are now moving towards us," Sue announced, "and that, quite fast!"

Well, by now we all noticed it too. But they were dispersing, and only one unit was moving towards us. The rest seemed as if they were preparing to encircle the globe.

"What fireworks!" Robbie jumped up with his arms raised.

The last thing I remember was everything starting to slow down, in extreme slow motion, like someone had pulled the plug. All the sudden, time started to shrink away. I looked around and observed everyone slowly gliding down, and falling asleep on their blankets. It was like when they give you narcotics at the hospital. No matter how hard you try to stay awake, things begin to slow down and eventually you're gone. It felt like a thousand arms were holding me up as I collapsed very gently down to the ground. I ended up in a deep sleep.

Chapter 9: Welcome to 'Freeland'

I smelled grass, and flowers. I used to like these dreams. Just lying in the grass, and looking up at the sky, or some nearby trees. It was warm, and the sun was high up. *Nice place*, I thought. *I haven't seen so much grass around where I live.* It's more desert-like in the south of Tenerife, and not so green, except for all the cacti and palm trees. *Don't wake up, it's a nice dream*, I told myself.

A butterfly was dancing in the air, as another was following him. Superb! You know how it is with dreams. When you're having a bad dream, going the wrong direction into something you don't want to experience, you make yourself wake up. You're not interested. But, when having positive dreams, you purposely try to fall back asleep to see where it's going. Most of the time you can't continue the nice dreams, as much as you'd like to; and that's how it was in this situation. I opened my eyes and saw the same field with flowers in front of my eyes, and the butterflies were still chasing each other, just like in my dream.

What's going on? I thought, as I bolted up like a rocket.

I started trying to reconstruct the past 24 hours in my mind. Robbie, Sue, and Melanie…up on Mount Teide, smoking some weed and watching the sunset while waiting for the full moon. Lovely discussions and Melanie snuggling up to me, and then the lights around the moon. That was all clear. Was it the weed? I didn't think so. We had smoked that same stuff before, and this time I had smoked even less. I wasn't one for smoking very much, as I was very sensitive spiritually, and was rather restrictive with myself. When taking the same amount as others, I would easily see, hear, and feel things around that no one else would notice, and it made me feel weird.

It couldn't be the weed, as I hadn't smoked much, I thought. *But what was it then?*

Suddenly, I remembered all these lights moving slowly towards us. I tried to remember further. One large group of lights was coming towards us, and then time suddenly shrunk and slowed down in slow-motion. That's the last thing I could remember before seeing the grass, flowers, and butterflies. *Had there been some invasion? And why was I here now, and where?* At least it was a lovely place, no doubt. I was laying amidst tall grass and flowers, surrounded by forest, and with no houses or civilization in sight. Just the kind of place I would usually be looking for to find peace and tranquillity.

I wasn't so tranquil now, though. A thousand thoughts were racing through my mind. *What happened to my friends? Where is this? And how can I contact my daughter? Maybe I should sleep some more, before this becomes a bad dream.* Then I heard voices coming from the forest.

Shit! I hope they are good people. Didn't I tell the girls I liked adventure? Well, here it was!

I hid in the tall grass, looking towards the place where the voices came from. I heard two people talking to each other: It was a man, and a woman.

"He should be here somewhere," I heard the woman say.

Who is the 'he' they're talking about, I wondered, as I hadn't seen anyone else here before they came. They started walking across the field in which I was doing my best to make myself unnoticed. I couldn't even see what they looked like. Maybe like aliens? But there was no real historic evidence in my mind to draw pictures from.

"Bernardo!" It was the woman calling.

I didn't answer. Now I was sort of scared too, although the voice sounded very friendly and calming.

"We're looking for you. We're here to help!" I heard the woman shout across the field. "We have some water and food for you," she continued, as if water and food would have made me any less scared at this point.

I slowly raised my head. They looked like hippies walking right out of the Woodstock festival, like some relics from the

60ties, only to be found in movies nowadays.

"Here; it's me," was about all that I could stutter, as I slowly raised my head out of the grass. They wore big smiles as they started running towards me with outstretched arms, like they wanted to hug me.

"It's so good to see you. We hope you have no bumps. We have tried to *transfer* you as gently as possible." They hugged me intensely, and all my resistance was gone. It felt so warm; like arriving home.

"Transfer?" I could hardly get out the word.

"Look, Bernardo, we have a lot of explaining to do, but here, drink some water first." They brought forth this old jug, and I drank from it. The water seemed very clean, fresh, and pure.

"We brought it from a nearby waterfall, that's why it's still so cool and refreshing," the woman explained.

"By the way, let us introduce ourselves. This is Paul, and my name is Mary."

"Nice to meet you. You apparently already know my name." I looked at them intently.

Their eyes seemed warm and loving, but somehow I couldn't stand to look in there for long; the light in their eyes was too bright. I looked down. I felt strange and very helpless, due to my ignorance of what was going on. Maybe the last time I had felt like that was when I was born; who knows.

"Who are you guys?"

"We're basically just souls like you. Except that we come from another place." That's the first time the dude opened his mouth.

"And from another time," Mary added. My jaw must have dropped a few inches.

"What did I get myself into, and why?" was all that I could muster up.

"It's a long story, Bernardo. We want to spend time with you explaining everything. We even brought food, so we can take our time."

I guess it was my turn to listen if I was going to get any

clarity on what had just happened. I watched the butterflies as they still fluttered around, just as before these people came. *They're still flying around, so these folks can't be evil*, I rationalized within myself. And why did I think that? I guess it had to do with my basic belief that no evil would befall me in life that wasn't permitted to happen by God or the universe. And I always thought that nature was very sensitive to evil people, but these butterflies were still there, and didn't seem to be worried.

I felt I should try to look some more into their eyes as the light in there was less blinding now. I noticed that his eyes were blue, like the ocean, with endless waves splashing against the rocks. They matched well with his long blond hair and beard. Hers seemed more like a green and lush mountain valley that led to some unknown destination. It wasn't the colour of their eyes, but what I saw in them, that gave me much peace all the sudden.

"We're just here to help," Mary said. "We're not here to harm".

"But what am I doing here?"

"Bernardo, this full moon had been appointed as the day to make another peaceful invasion of Earth, as has been done at several occasions in the past. We started doing this a while back, and since it's proven to be helpful, we keep doing it."

"Yes, it's the first stage of an experiment, to see how you humans react when coming into a better, and more loving environment," Paul added. "We all felt like something needed to be done. Things have gotten to be too bad down there."

"That's true. Some of my friends and I had been hoping for something like this to happen," I started chiming in on this challenging discussion. *You better stay quiet though, and instead take in all they need to tell you*, I ended up telling myself.

I was reminded of all the talks I'd had on various occasions with Robbie, and others, regarding the possibility of aliens coming to help us. *So yes, so far so good*, I thought.

"So you guys came in those lights we saw last night?" I said matter-of-factly. They smiled at me.

"We know we've chosen the right people. You guys

answer most of the questions yourselves."

"But I'm here alone. So far I haven't seen anyone except you guys."

"We are going to explain all that to you now Bernardo, are you ready?" By now I most definitely was. "Let's sit down and make ourselves comfortable, we have a lot of explaining to do."

"You are not the only one who was transferred last night. Hundreds of people have landed here along with you, while others have already been here for a while. Many more would be very deserving of coming to see this place too. But, it's in part a logistical problem. And second, for many people this would be too much of a shock at this point in their lives. That's why we only bring a few hundred people at once."

I could understand their point, immediately realizing that Sue and Melanie probably weren't going to be here, neither Birgit, as they had all expressed a certain fear of aliens. But, maybe Robbie was?

"Yes, it's as Paul says. Most people are not spiritually ready for the time being, and maybe not emotionally either. However, they might come here at a later point in their lives."

"So, the people I love aren't here?" I felt this huge sadness coming over me.

"Cheer up, Bernardo, we have thought of that. Didn't you say that unpredictable is sort of the opposite of boring? Look forward to finding out! We don't want to remove all the surprise elements from your life." This made me smile.

"Well, I did say that a while back to Birgit. Have you guys been listening in on my conversations and thoughts?" They looked at me like they'd done nothing harmful.

"We know a lot more about you than you think, Bernardo," they answered. "For now you will be led to all the other people that have been transferred to this place."

"You mean to say that this is supposed to be my new home? I mean, did I die on Earth?" I thought this was a valid question.

"Good question, Bernardo, but no, you didn't die. This can be your new home if you wish. Some people have stayed ever since they arrived here. But, perhaps you will miss your loved ones and will want to go back, as many have already done. You won't enjoy staying here if there is heartache. And, as we know you, you will probably miss certain individuals. Some people want to stay here for good, while others prefer to go back. There are no negative repercussions for anyone going back. This opportunity is all out of love, and not by any means of coercion." Mary looked at me, and I could see that endless green valley in her eyes again.

"The idea is that those going back might have a positive effect on their surroundings, and the world, after they've made this trip here. Others prefer to stay, as they have become too tired of the world down there. It's all good, Bernardo, it's all good."

"That does sound great," I said. "Where do you guys get such good ideas from?" They both laughed.

"The reasons for choosing to transfer you were that we have been following your spiritual development for a long time, and have concluded that you would probably like it here, at least for a visit. You have yourself expressed such a desire. We felt that this would be the right time, enabling you to get a lot further in your spiritual growth. Therefore, people who seem to be ready for this get a chance to have a look, and experience first-hand what this world here is all about."

"What is it all about?"

"It's a lot of things, Bernardo. In "Freeland", as this place is called, you are going to find people from all walks of life."

"I can't wait to meet them. It sounds exciting." I was getting intrigued by their ideas. *Even if they'd somehow transfer me back right after this, I'd already had a great time.*

"There are people with religious background, others with no such background whatsoever, as well as folks of all colours and nations."

That makes sense, I pondered.

"The only credo here in *Freeland* is: 'No greed'. We could have come up with 'Love' as the only standard here, but love can mean a lot of things, and can be confusing in its interpretation. That's why we limited the law here to be simply 'No greed'. There will be plenty of food here for everyone's existence. We even have a small house for you which you'll get to see later. It's as Mahatma Gandhi said: 'Enough for everyone's need, but not for anyone's greed.'"

She paused. I felt bad for her having to do all this explaining, while Paul stayed mostly quiet. I guess he had other functions or maybe he was going to take over the explaining later.

"We have made sure to only bring people here whom we have observed as being non-greedy. We don't want another selfish world here. One out there is already one too much."

Now it seemed it was Paul's turn: "We don't look at having some wants, such as wanting a guitar or piano, or wanting to obtain certain music or books, as a problem. We know you all have your little wants and needs. We're talking about real greed, like exploiting the poor or stealing from others, or being unwilling to share from the riches one has accumulated. Violence is another 'no go', but we don't want to make too many laws. We have carefully selected only people with no history of greedy and violent behaviour."

"In other words, all the things that make the world so unpleasant these days, such as greed and violence, are totally out of sight here, and don't even exist. But, of course, should anything greedy or violent occur, the person enacting such things would be expelled and transferred back to where greed and violence are rampant."

"That's amazing!" I said in great surprise. "So if someone isn't greedy, but respectful to others, they can stay here forever?"

"Forever is a long time, Bernardo." They both smiled.

"But then why didn't you guys just take over the whole world?"

"That's a very valid question," Paul answered. "In reality, we weren't even that enthusiastic about this big project at first. We all needed to leave loved ones to be part of this mission. It's more of a must than a desire, because humanity was supposed to be left alone to make its choices, good choices, within the fabulous environment they were given. But by now mankind has messed things up a whole lot, to say the least. That's why this project was decided on, and has gotten those of us who volunteered extremely busy."

They must be working hard to make this possible, I realized.

"I'm sure that you will agree with us that the industrial revolution was the beginning of the real downfall of mankind. That is not to say that an old-fashioned telephone and fridge aren't useful. But what about all these other things the world started producing, and advertising on TV to make people feel like they would need all that stuff? It's the wrong road, because human intelligence should be used to solve the problems of starvation and injustice; teaching people to get back to farming instead of moving to factories; to love and share instead of abuse and hate."

It all sounded so much like some of our discussions we'd had down by *the rocks*, and I felt right at home.

"Yeah, I'm all with you. My friends and I have been saying that kind of stuff all along."

They chuckled. "That's exactly why you're here, Bernardo. We hope you will like it. We won't be staying around here to tell you guys what to do. As a matter of fact, as soon as this conversation is over, we will disappear and you won't see us again."

"Really?" I probably sounded a bit disappointed, because they seemed nice, like people you'd want to keep as close friends. "But what if I have more questions?"

"Then you should ask them now. But the other folks we have brought to this place have also been asking us and our friends questions. They are getting answers too and you should be able to piece the important parts together."

I couldn't have imagined such a turn of events in the wildest of my imaginations.

"So, do you have any more questions before we go?"

"Oh, I would have so many, but I'm still in a state of shock due to my transfer here, and trying to figure out what this all means…But yes, one thing I would like to ask before you guys disappear: How come I was born into the world, gathering some superb childhood memories of kind people, surrounded by a beauty of nature that is second to none, only to learn later that I was surrounded by a world so cruel, hateful, unloving, and destructive?"

"I know it's weird, Bernardo," Mary explained. "Realizing that they were born into a very greedy and selfish world is difficult for many. Pain and suffering have become the daily bread for people, including nature and wildlife. It was an experiment, but the experiment has failed. It's now time for something new."

"This project has been in preparation for quite a while. A variety of climates have been set up here, for things to grow all year around. We have the same animals and vegetation as what you are used to, so that you will feel more at home."

"You guys are amazing."

"We are love, Bernardo, and one day you will be love too. Your road has already led you to become a more loving person, and you will keep on learning as you go."

"That all sounds great. And how far away is this place from planet Earth?" *I don't think they will like to answer that one*, I realized.

"We can't tell you that, Bernardo, but it's all taken care of and nothing to worry about. You will be able to see your loved ones any time, because when you start missing them too much, you will be transferred back. Your wish will be our command, so to speak. All you will need to do is send us a message, like a prayer, or some kind of request."

"And, when I return, I won't be able to come back here again?"

"That's a good question, Bernardo. Anyone who starts missing this place too much will be able to come back. We don't mind people going back and forth."

That is such a tolerant attitude, I thought. "And what should I tell people who ask me about where I have been during my absence?"

"There won't be any such questions because there won't be any such absence. We have put everyone around you to sleep. So, no matter how long you will decide to be here, you will be right back there in your sleeping-bag on top of the mountain when the others wake up. They won't notice you've been anywhere else. And the clock will have remained at the same point as when you left, at least for you and those being brought here."

"That's brilliant! How do you guys do that?"

"We have another concept of time, but it's difficult and somewhat unnecessary to explain to you right now."

"I imagine this place isn't somewhere on the globe," I said, sort of knowingly. I wouldn't even have wanted to know how far away from my loved ones I was. Since that question was more of a rhetorical one, I figured I'd better ask one more, before our question and answer time would be over.

"I do have one more question. I mean, why would any aliens even want to visit planet Earth? There must be more peaceful places to visit."

I looked at Mary, and just one glimpse at her eyes made it clear to me that they were here on a mission of love. "You've answered that question yourself, Bernardo. We're just trying to help, that's all. It's hard work trying to find out who would benefit from coming here next."

"That must be a lot of work indeed. It's strange, because somehow I always had the feeling that my thoughts were being watched, and if they were selfish, it somehow didn't feel right."

"Look at is as gift: Someone's protecting you from harm, but with you at the controls."

"We do have another extraordinary gift for you before we leave," she said, while pulling out this radiant clear crystal from her bag, and putting it in my hand. "This is yours, Bernardo. It will be your biggest help around here. It serves as a light in the dark, but will also stop shining when you go the wrong direction. It will always show you the way back to your house, no matter where you go. We don't want people to get lost around here."

"Wow, this is gorgeous! Looks like one of those my grandfather used to find while climbing up in the alps. Can I keep it?"

"It's yours! It will lead you to the meeting place where everyone having arrived today will be gathering. Many of those who have already been here will be there as well, to welcome you and help you get adjusted to this place."

"After the party, your crystal will direct you to your new home," Paul continued. "Your own personal telephone number is engraved in it, if you look closely. It's basically your date of birth, with a few letters attached to it, as some people will obviously share the same date of birth. That way, when you get to know people you have a means to contact each other again. We have installed regular telephone lines to all the houses."

"You guys are real freaks! You think of everything, even telephones."

"We don't think of telephones as an evil invention. They can be quite helpful in connecting people."

"Bernardo, there is one important thing we must ask of you before leaving. Whenever you will go back to your former environment, please don't tell anyone what you will see and experience here. Keep it to yourself, unless you find out someone has visited here as well."

"But what about some people 'spilling the beans', giving this information out accidentally or on purpose. Will they be punished?"

It was Paul who answered this delicate question: "Well, we aren't into punishment. And it's not such a big deal if someone doesn't abide by our wish. People probably wouldn't believe it anyway if they'd hear about it."

"But it's better for people on Earth not to hear about *Freeland*," she continued. "We don't want there to be any panic breaking out. And, as you know, mankind tries to destroy all things beautiful once they find out about their existence. That's why we prefer for you guys not to talk about your stay here once you'll get back."

That was all too much for me. I just rolled back on the

grass and looked up into the sky. I probably shouldn't have smoked that weed last night. I shook my head a couple of times, and then sat up again.

"So this is real?"

"It is very real, Bernardo, and you are going to find out over the next few days just how real this is."

"I still can't believe that I'm so blessed to be a part of this. After all, I'm nobody special."

"Everyone is special! You are somebody special too, otherwise, we wouldn't have brought you here," Mary said.

"Yes," Paul added. "We find it too difficult to judge who has the edge on someone else, because each individual has their strong points and weak points. We wish the whole world would be able to come here, but we have decided to just bring a few people at a time, and then see how they handle being here and how it affects them."

"Well, I certainly won't miss the greed and strife, but I may miss a couple of people too much, after having been here for a while."

"That's understandable, Bernardo. You can let us know, and we'll arrange for your trip back. Anyway, it will get dark soon, as the sun here begins to set, just as yours does down on Earth. It's time for us to leave this place."

"You won't see us again, but we will see you. We're praying for you, and hope you will make the most of your time here in *Freeland*."

They gave me another one of those warmest of hugs, and then, with tears in their eyes, they left towards the same place they had come from. I couldn't believe it as I saw them crying for me, as if I were their son or daughter.

Mary turned around one last time: "At the end of the party tonight, just point your crystal and it will lead you to your house. We love you so much; you are such a sweet soul. Pass that sweetness on to others. The world needs it." Now it was my turn to start tearing up.

"I will miss you both. I hope to see you again someday."

They waved goodbye as they left, and I could still hear

their voices in the distance, until finally all went quiet. By quiet, I mean very quiet, even the birds I'd heard before seemed to have gone to sleep as soon as it had started to get dark.

After they left, I didn't feel totally alone. There was something special about that crystal in my hands. It started to shine, as I pointed it in the direction in which they had disappeared. It seemed to have a life and purpose of its own, with strong and comforting energy flowing through it. And most importantly, being a companion to this *lonely traveller.*

Chapter 10: Big party in the sky

I was glad to get some movement after having sat there. I started walking in the direction in which the crystal was leading, but, of course, my new *friends* weren't there anymore. *They must have changed into some other form of energy, and gone off to their next assignment,* I thought.

The crystal shone its light on a little path that went through the forest, so I just continued in that direction. It shone so brightly that I could see the small track winding its way through tall pine trees before me. I always loved crystals, and this one was breathtakingly beautiful. I wondered where its energy came from, since it obviously didn't run on batteries. I could even feel it warm my hands.

I continued walking, breathing in the warm forest air. Dusk is a wonderful time: the slow change from day to night; from warm to cold; and the new sounds of nature that awaken with the darkness. I felt hungry and realized that I had forgotten to take some of the food which my hosts had brought along. *There will probably be some food at the place I'm heading to,* I contemplated.

I hiked through the forest until I came to its edge. I found myself on a hilltop, which opened the view to a valley so big that I couldn't see the end of it. It was stunning. There were so many stars out, all seeming to smile at me, and some sort of a moon was illuminating the whole scene ahead of me. I could quite clearly see the outline of the valley, which started out quite narrow, but widened further off in the distance, with a river flowing through it. The scene reminded me a lot of the alps, especially after detecting some snow on top of the peaks in the distance. It was very fascinating indeed, and so I just stood there for a few minutes, taking in all the wonderful vibes.

Suddenly, I noticed a deer standing on my left, staring at me; unafraid. *I'm sure they must feel much better around here, with noone chasing them around and trying to kill them*, I thought. I went over to caress him, which was appreciated. The amazing thing was that the deer started walking in front of me, like he'd be trying to show me the way to something. I heard the splashing of water and sure enough, we arrived at a big waterfall coming down over some cliffs. It was the beginning of the stream that would later turn into a river, flowing through the whole valley. I drank some fresh water and so did the deer.

After coming to me for some more caressing, he turned back into the direction we had come from, but not without turning his head one more time, as if wanting to say goodbye. I felt like there was some sort of telepathic interaction between the two of us. He held his head still, and looked at me for a moment. I could see a forest, and animals moving around, like in a movie. Perhaps, if I'd taken the time, I might have seen his whole life in there. I wondered if he had also been transferred here, but there wasn't time to get into this now as I needed to get to the gathering.

The next thing I recalled was a light approaching from out of the forest to my right. It was another person with their hands firmly clasped around their crystal.

"Hi, my name is Bernardo. I was brought here from Spain. It seems like we might be headed in the same direction!"

"I hope so! My name's Serena," the young lady introduced herself. "Before landing here, I lived in London. I am pleased to meet you, Bernardo. I'm still quite nervous, but excited at the same time, but maybe just a tiny bit scared to walk through this dark forest alone. However, if I understood correctly, there are only sweet people in this part of the world."

"Well, Serena, I don't think this is part of the world as we know it."

We gave each other a big hug, and continued our walk in the direction in which our crystals were guiding. "Were you also met by two people?"

"Yes, by two ladies: Marisha and Catherine. I always feel

intimidated by guys. I guess they knew that."

"That's brilliant! They are very considerate."

"Indeed, Bernardo. They also told me that I can leave this place anytime I wish to go back, which I might do later as I don't think my girlfriend will be here." It seemed that the information she had gotten corresponded to the things I'd heard from them.

"I've been told the same thing, and it makes me feel at ease, knowing that I can choose how long I'd like to stay. Oh, by the way, I forgot to ask them one thing. Do you know if we are given any type of special powers?" I was referring to the experience I'd just had with that deer.

"I actually asked them that question, Bernardo. They explained that we will be given more love, and that would be powerful enough. They added that we will be a lot more sensitive spiritually while here, because of the unpolluted surroundings."

"That makes sense. I don't want any special powers; it might go to my head."

"Can I hold your hand while we walk in the dark?" she asked.

I took her hand, as we headed down a wider road, leading to an area in the valley from where we could see some lights. We continued to make our way through fields of grass and flowers. It was a vegetation like you'd see in many parts of Europe. It had gotten colder, and I put my sweater back on.

"I hope everyone has a sweater with them," Serena said with some concern. "I was told that there would be some storehouse where we'll find everything we need. They've spent much time in preparation for this project, they said."

"Oh, they're just so loving and caring; if only people around the world were like that too! I think we can learn a lot from them. This is certainly a unique event in the history of the world. Although I'm not sure if history will ever know about this, because we're not meant to talk about our experience to anyone; if we happen to go back."

"I know, Bernardo. I would have never thought such a

thing would ever happen. I'm very excited to be a part of it."

After strolling through hills and fields, we arrived at a hamlet which consisted of a few wooden houses, some of which had their lights on. It even had a name, scrawled down on a small wooden post at its entrance, which read: "Valle Hermosa." We noticed a herd of deer grazing on the left side of the village, where the meadows met the forest. As our crystals shone into their eyes, we could see them reflecting the light back at us. It looked so pretty and mysterious at the same time.

As we reached a main road, there were more travellers with their crystals in their hands joining us from every side of the valley. We introduced ourselves and hugged each other, starting lively conversations as we continued the journey. "Do I know you from somewhere?" was the question I heard quite a few times, as many of the people looked somewhat familiar to each other.

We spent the following hour making our way further along the river, to where the valley widened. A first major village we passed was called "Fiume Grande", a name matching the river there, which by now had become quite big. I had noticed a lot of small streams flowing down from the mountains and valleys on each side.

We were all glad to finally reach our goal: A large opening with a massive gathering of people. "Plaza Mayor", it said. *Amazing*, I thought, *the names of villages and places seem to be in either Italian or Spanish, which are my two favourite languages.* I noticed various roads leading down towards this central place, with more arrivals making their way down from the various hills where they had landed.

The scene was illuminated by lanterns with candles, giving out a warm light. Our crystals continued to give off some light too, so we could see whom we were talking to.

I attempted to stay close to the various people I had met on my way here, but as everyone started mingling and getting into conversations with other people, I eventually couldn't see them anymore. People were getting to know each other, laughing and having a great time. I was relieved to see some restaurants, and since my stomach was growling, I made my way there. "The Italian Restaurant" caught my attention.

"You can also find Thai, Indian, Asian and South American food," someone informed me.

Italian food sounded just fine for now. The restaurant was offering grilled vegetables with pasta. I served myself some, adding pesto to it. It was delicious, as was the local red wine I drank along with it. Some soft music could be heard in the background, just loud enough so as not to interrupt the conversations the diners were having.

I met some folks from the United States who were sitting at the same table. They were interested in my stories from Europe, as they had wanted to travel there. The initial shock after our arrival seemed to have given way to a very relaxed atmosphere, as we were sharing various adventures and stories from our lives.

"Look how relaxed and excited everyone is; like they'd been hoping to come to a place like this forever." I was talking to a young lady called Janis, from Michigan.

"True! I think many of my friends would have deserved to come here as well, judging by their beliefs. But I think for some of them it would be too much of a change from their daily routine," she said. "My friend Kevin made it here and I'm just so excited about that." She introduced me to him.

"We have had a relationship for some time; not a very close one, but I think that will change now," Kevin said as they snuggled up to each other. I noticed that quite a few people seemed to have met their friends already, and were rejoicing over it.

"I would like to get to know someone who has been living here for a while. Do you know anyone?" I asked him.

"Yes, of course!"

He went over to a group of people, and came back with a guy who introduced himself as Eddie. He told me that he had been travelling around a lot here, in search of precious stones and crystals, which he'd trade in for food.

"They are easy to trade in, and I even found out that when you decide to go back, they are transferred back with you" Eddie explained.

'

"Really?"

"Yes, if it's not done with a greedy attitude. Some things you find here, or even stuff you create, will be transferred back with you once you decide to go back. We know about it because some people have already returned for a second time."

"That means if I create some paintings here they might be transferred back to my house on Earth?"

"Most definitely, Bernardo; whatever isn't done out of greed. Everyone should evaluate their hearts and motives, as we don't want to sadden the aliens. They've been so good to us."

That sounded incredible. We exchanged our phone numbers, which he wrote down using a wooden pen and some paper.

"These are both made here," Eddie explained, replying to the astonished look on my face. "The paper is made by a French guy who started a paper mill, producing paper from hemp."

I smelled the paper. "From the Valley of Hemp", he said with a big smile. "My friend Robbie would love that valley!" I exclaimed. "Wow, and look at this pencil!"

"Yes, isn't it nice? There is a guy in the 'Valley of Carpentry' who makes those. You'll find them at the market. You should visit that valley, it's extremely interesting. Only old trees are cut down, the ones that have either dried out, or are about to fall anyways. And, for every such tree, a new tree is planted. I've met some real forest freaks there who care passionately about nature and the trees."

"I have a question for you, since you seem to travel a lot around this island, or whatever it is."

"It is an island; I've been to every corner. It takes about four full days to get from one end to the other by carriage. The climate varies in different parts, which is great, because certain things grow better in certain places." That already answered my basic question, as I had wanted to know how big this place was, and if it had a beginning and an end.

He continued: "When you get to your house, there is a map of *Freeland* on the wall. It was made by someone who had already made maps down on Earth, so it's very relatable and exact. It depicts everything: the roads, mountains, villages, and valleys. There is a 'Valley of Rice', a 'Valley of Coffee', and the 'Valley of Wine', just to mention a few. The name indicates the main resources that are being produced there. We also have regions. The hill over there for example is in the 'Region of Mangoes and Avocados.' The local markets make it possible to obtain products from other parts. Some people enjoy trading, and they're the ones who spend their time bringing stuff around. That's not bad, since there is no greed involved. It's great!"

"Indeed! Thanks so much for filling me in on some of these things. I feel so thankful to have been able to come here and experience this!"

"Yes, Bernardo, we all are greatly blessed. It is nice to have you here. Please give me a call once you have made yourself at home. I would like to see the paintings that you'll make. Maybe you would be interested to exchange art for some crystals?"

"You mean you have a collection?"

"Of course, it was my passion before coming here. I go to caves, and climb up rocks in search of them. I have never encountered such a good place for finding crystals as here."

"Well, I would certainly want to pay you a visit, and get to see your beauties. And yes, I will bring a couple of paintings along, as soon as I have finished some."

"People interested in forests, wood, and carpentry would probably have their house in the 'Valley of Carpentry', while someone like me might have theirs in some place near gorgeous views," I speculated.

"Yes, it works somewhat like that, but it also has to do with placing you near your friends. Usually it's just the perfect place. However, one can also choose to move to another house if the one assigned isn't suitable for some reason. You would just need to go around and find one that's not inhabited. Your phone number goes with you, and can be used at the new place as well."

"You don't need to ask the aliens, or someone else?"

"There are no aliens here, Bernardo; they stay out of this. And you don't need to ask anyone else, there are no governors here. We all take care of each other, with no politicians or gurus to rule over us. If a house is free, it's free to move into."

"In other words: A society built on love."

"Exactly. I don't even like to hear the word 'society' anymore, as it is so often connected to corruption, selfishness, exploitation, and so on."

My head was spinning, and I felt much higher than high. The feeling of being lonely here hadn't even appeared as there were *friends* all over the place. It didn't seem to matter if you knew someone from before coming here or not. Everyone became a friend as soon as you started talking to them.

The party went until late into the night. I began feeling tired. "They told me that my crystal would guide me to my little house, did they tell you the same?" I asked Janis and Kevin.

"That's the same we heard, and we're getting rather tired too, so we are going to go and verify that now."

"It works," Eddie said. "I'm sure each of you will find your house. But I need to inform you that there are no more carriages for public transport at this hour."

"But what if my house ends up being on the other end of the island? I'm already quite tired," I sighed.

"No worry, Bernardo! Every house is like a free hotel and has a guestroom. We're all open to help each other, as it does happen that one may get stuck somewhere and be unable to make it home for the night."

"Every house a free hotel? That's truly fascinating." I thought how nice it was to have some of the old-timers here at this gathering, assisting us new arrivals with needed information and advice.

After parting with big hugs, I now looked forward to start the search for my bed.

Chapter 11: My new home

As I raised my crystal to look for direction, it led me to one of the main roads leading gently up a nearby hill. The road wasn't paved, but was obviously used by famers with their carriages. I had hoped not to find any modern equipment here and I wasn't disappointed, as there obviously were no cars.

I enjoyed the cool air, which was at a lovely temperature for this time of night. I could still faintly hear the music from the *Plaza Mayor* playing softly. It was very peaceful, and not loud and aggressive as I had been used to from *La Roca*.

After the first couple of curves uphill, I stopped to have a look at the scenery. As the moon and the stars shone brighter here, the valley and surrounding hills could be seen quite well, and I noticed some villages on the opposite side of the hill. I assumed that those on my side of the valley wouldn't be much higher up.

I saw various lights dispersing from where the party had taken place, as people took off in search of their homes. Some of the lights followed up behind me, on the same road I had taken. I waited to see who'd come up behind me as I didn't want to walk alone. The light got closer and I heard someone humming a song. The voice sounded very familiar.

"Robbie?" I shouted.

"Bernardo, is that you?"

I ran back down a piece of the road as he ran towards me, and we fell into each other's arms. What a reunion that was!

"From the top of the Teide into a new world, Bernardo! Who would have ever thought of such a thing?"

"Yes. I'm so thrilled that you're here. This must be one of the best days of my life. I'm not even tired anymore!"

We had somewhat suspected that we might meet each other, and it was a very emotional moment for both of us. As we made our way up the hill, we shared our encounters we'd had with the aliens, as well as the people we'd met since then.

"Do you think they will miss us at home?" I asked Robbie.

"I don't think so. I was told that noone would even realize that we had ever left, once we'd get back. I've never been flying so high in my life, even though I haven't touched a joint tonight."

"You'll probably be interested to hear that there is a 'Valley of hemp', as I was told."

"That sounds great! I also heard of other exciting places to discover, even a 'Surfer's Paradise'. And you might be delighted to know that they are the 'Freeland alps' here.

I hadn't heard about that, but was already planning an excursion in my mind.

We had reached the top of the hill and were now looking over various valleys and hills with high mountains in the back. The valley down below was gradually widening into a plain, at the end of which we saw the 'ocean', reflecting the moonlight. We were both spellbound by this view.

"Wow, that's very impressive! That's where *Surfer's Paradise* must be."

We also noticed the climate being much more mild here, with palm trees and cacti, like you'd find somewhere along the Mediterranean coast.

Arriving at a crossing with street signs, one of them pointed to the right and read: "Bellezza". That's a lovely Italian name for a village, meaning "Beauty". We soon reached the place and could make out houses and lights. White stone houses were lined up beside each other and dispersed all over the hill, allowing for each house to have a view over the valley. Lanterns were illuminating the way to the front doors.

"This place is economical; there are no street lights," noticed an observant Robbie. "I had always wondered why we need street lights on Earth; they use up so much energy. But then again, with all the violence going on, I can understand why some people prefer to have them."

We had turned a couple more corners when Robbie's light suddenly went out in front of a gorgeous little house. "Robbie's home", was carved into a wooden sign on the front door.

"I think this might be my place. I sure hope yours isn't too far." Since I suspected mine might be next to his, I walked a bit further, and sure enough, my 'lamp' went out at the neighbouring house. "Bernardo's home" said the sign on the door before me. We were both very thankful to be neighbours for the first time.

We decided to first have a look at Robbie's, so we passed through the front door, which wasn't locked. Since people here don't steal, it makes no sense to have to lock the door. It had some nice Tibetan bells hanging outside, so that visitors could announce their arrival. I couldn't resist giving them a push to hear their magnificent sound.

"Welcome to my new home!" We entered a large living room, and Robbie just burst out in screams.

"Look, Bernardo, my surfboard and sail is here!" He was jumping up and down for joy. He found that all kinds of things had been transferred here from his place in Tenerife, including his guitar.

"Ha, Bernardo, even the painting which you made for my birthday is hanging on the wall!"

"No problem for them to transfer physical matter, it seems."

"Yes, that's what it looks like. And, even my hi-fi and my records are here." He put on his Jimmy Hendrix record. It certainly matched all that we were feeling at that moment. "Just missing the foxy ladies now, Bernardo; but I'm sure with time they will appear as well." The only thing that wasn't there was a TV, but we didn't miss that at all. We discovered an old-fashioned radio, which Robbie turned on.

"Welcome to your new home, dear friend! On this radio-station we are continuously broadcasting news, events, reports, discussions, interviews, music and interesting information about *Freeland* around the clock. You'll find no news from the planet you came from, as things won't have changed there for the better once you'll get back. You'll find programmes in diverse languages, as well as different styles of music to listen to. It's nice to have you with us! If you have any positive news to share, please call us on the following number. This is your moderator, Johnny, from *Radio Freeland*."

We were speechless for a moment and felt so loved and cared for by our hosts. Robbie got excited over his little eating corner, all made of natural wood, with an open, fully-furnished kitchen. There was a living room with a fireplace, a master bedroom, plus a smaller guest room. I was studying the information on the board by the entrance. The village market wasn't a business, it said, but a place to exchange products from our gardens, or other self-made creations, such as handicraft, clothing, books, and art. Services could also be traded in for goods.

"Wow. I can even trade in my paintings for food and such," I noticed excitedly.

"Oh, and this must be the map of *Freeland* which Eddie had mentioned". It had a red circle to indicate where exactly we were located on the map, in *Bellezza*. I had always loved studying maps. In the meantime, Robbie went to look for something drinkable in his fridge, and he found some *Freeland beer*.

I found *Surfer's Paradise* on the map and Robbie was overjoyed. "They knew where to place me, we're not far from there!"

"Let's celebrate with a beer. It says 'Made with love in Wheat Valley'. They apparently didn't only grow wheat there, but hop and malt as well." The beer tasted excellent, very natural and aromatic, and we were thankful that there were several bottles in the fridge.

There was some other interesting advice hanging on the board, such as how to dispose our green garbage by composting it in the garden; what to do in case of fire; or where there was a doctor should any illness occur. There was, evidently, no number for any police, as that was not needed here.

We also discovered a large storage room beneath the house, filled with avocados, mangoes, eggplant, zucchini, and tomatoes, which were probably harvested from the garden outside. Other items, like coffee, bread, rice, pasta, dry beans, nuts and some cereals were already there, so that we would have enough food to last until we could bring our own products to the market.

"I wonder how the surroundings look in the daytime, Bernardo. It must be fabulous."

We went over to my house, which had a similar layout as Robbie's. My biggest surprise was that my favourite paintings were hanging on the walls; including the one Jasi had made for me at school. My painting equipment was here as well, and I was glad I had just bought some more recently. Also present was my guitar, congas, as well as all kinds of photographs and memories. I opened the fridge and found freshly pressed orange juice, and some vegetable pies.

"The aliens thought of everything, Robbie. I wonder if they live inside my head."

By now, it was so late, and with both of us feeling exhausted from this eventful day, we wanted nothing more than to go to sleep. Wishing each other goodnight, Robbie went over to his house. Before getting to bed myself, I noticed a list of people who had lived in this house before. There was a request at the top to add my name there too. It served as sort of a historic inventory of who had lived in this house. I wrote my name down, along with my birthday. Who knew if any of my friends might stay here later, and it might bring a smile to their face when they see that I'd lived in this house as well.

The views from the living room and master bedroom were extraordinary. Both rooms were fitted with doors accessing the terrace, from which you had a view over the whole valley. On the terrace was a pergola with grapevines growing all over it, offering plenty of shade, in case temperatures were to rise. The villages on the other side of the valley were shimmering like stars in the sky. Robbie and I had already spoken about how we would love to explore some of the regions and valleys that were shown on the map, and I was looking forward to some exciting adventures. I went to my bedroom, put my crystal down on the night-table, and let my head drop onto a very soft pillow.

'Fabricated with feathers from ducks who died of natural causes', it read on the tag. I liked the way things were explained and labelled here, so that you could know the origin of each product.

"Thanks to God and the universe for bringing me to this wonderful place," I whispered, as I fell fast asleep.

The sun was already high up in the sky when my eyes opened. I jumped up: *I want to see the view.* I went out onto the terrace and looked over the whole valley. On the other side, I could see mountains behind hills, and I could distinctly see all the villages on the other side of our valley, where the *Fiume Grande* river was flowing through lush agricultural land. Down below, I noticed the place where the welcome party had been held last night, as well as the dark blue ocean in the distance.

I had a look around the outside area. In between the houses, I spotted vegetable and herb gardens, fruit trees, and in front of my house there was a rock garden with flowers, cacti and succulents. There were further terraces below my house, with various fruit trees and garden plots, all connected by stairs.

A fresh breeze rushed through my hair, and I felt so free. There was no noise, except for a few birds coming over to eat the crumbs from my table. It was very different from what I was used to, with people rushing to their jobs, cars and busses speeding around, and the hectic noise of a materialistic society. I didn't miss the world I'd left behind. There was no such rush here, and it was so pleasantly peaceful.

I went over to the kitchen and hoped to get myself some coffee. There stood an old-fashioned Italian coffee-maker, the kind that can be put directly on the stove. The coffee smelled great, and I wondered if it was being produced here. 'Produced with love in the Coffee Valley', was written on the glass container.

Happily finding no household equipment made from plastics, I examined the cleaning products and body soap, which appeared to all be natural, made in the 'Valley of Herbs'. *That must be a great valley to visit as well, and to watch the various artisans produce these natural products*, I thought. As I stepped out onto the terrace with my cup of coffee, I found Robbie had come out of his bedroom and was enjoying the sights.

"Good morning Bernardo. What a gorgeous day! It's awesome to have you as my neighbour. Did you sleep well? I slept so peacefully and with all my worries far away."

"I've got the same feeling here. I was very tired, but I feel incredibly refreshed now. And yes, there doesn't seem to be any kind of hectic life going on out here. No cars or planes browsing around, and no one trying to see who can work harder than their neighbour. It's a very calm and unhurried atmosphere. It would be hard to find any place in the world where one can experience this."

"And just how far away from Earth are we? Has anyone told you?"

"I did ask that, but they didn't want to give any information about the location of this place. We might in fact be lightyears away from home, who knows. I guess they don't want any information regarding the location of this place to leak out, or else some humans might be quick to start sending rockets here. And you can just imagine how peaceful this place might stay if humans were to export their materialism and industrialization here."

"Yes, Bernardo. It gives me a lot of peace, knowing that humans will never find out where this place is." I went over to his terrace with my coffee in hand, and bringing along one for my friend.

"One thing I noticed is that there is a gardening journal where everything is marked down, such as when the trees were last pruned, what would need to be done next, how often they need to be watered, etc. I find that very helpful," Robbie informed me.

"I've seen that too. Our predecessors did a good job in

writing it all down. We'll need to follow suit. I'm not so good at gardening, but I'd like to learn."

"Few of us really had much training in gardening, but I'm sure there will be someone who's good at it, and able to tell us what to do, so that our gardens and plantations will continue to flourish. I actually enjoy gardening and used to help my dad a lot back when I was a kid," he explained.

"I'll be looking for a gardener who would do my garden in exchange for a painting, so I can have my time available to make new ones."

"That's a good idea, Bernardo. And I would like to go down to *Surfer's Paradise*, in hope of being able to give some surfing lessons there."

It felt so different than down on Earth, where one always has some appointments lined up, and so much to do, with all the stress that is artificially created to keep everyone so busy that many people rarely find the time to even think, and with very little time left for their hobbies and passion.

"I can hear a lot more animals and birds here, as there is no human noise obstructing them."

"That's true, Robbie. I noticed this morning how the sound of the animals is so much more intense here. There are probably a lot of wild animals around as well, since no one hunts them down." That was explicitly forbidden here, and was classified as violence, resulting in immediate expulsion back to Earth.

"Have you noticed what a pleasant cool breeze we have up here? No need for expensive air-conditioning. I love how there are practically no electrical appliances here: No TV, vacuum-cleaner, or big coffee-machines. There is just a small fridge and an old-fashioned telephone, on which it says 'for calls within *Freeland* only.'"

"I found a 'Valley of Ecological Energy' on the map. There must be some technical and environment-oriented freaks living there, helping to produce the small amount of electricity needed, which was being produced solely by wind- and water-mills." Robbie had also heard of that.

After having had some breakfast, finishing the delicious vegetable pie that was in the fridge, we decided to go on a walk to explore our village as well as the surroundings. The hills behind were saturated with houses, orchards, and gardens. It was hard to tell if they were all inhabited, but we passed by quite a few people waving at us from different terraces. We also crossed some folks walking by on the streets, and introduced ourselves. We were very excited to find a village bakery, and stepped in to see what was being offered. Regrettably, we hadn't brought anything to trade with.

"Pepe is my name. I come from mainland Spain, from Madrid," the jolly baker explained.

"Madrid? My daughter lives there!" I said.

"I've been here for about one year, and honestly don't miss anyone down there. So, I choose to stay on."

He seemed to be around the same age as us, and was very excited to hear we came from the Canary Islands, as he used to visit there quite often. He offered several types of bread in his shop, as well as a few fruit cakes.

"I'm the only baker on this side of the hill. People come from all around; especially those who are not too good at baking themselves."

"That's us!" Robbie laughed.

"If you can tell me what goods or services you offer, we can make a friendly deal."

"Bernardo is a painter and makes the most dazzling paintings. And I'm planning on giving surf lessons down at *Surfer's Paradise*. We do a little bit of gardening on the side, our plantations producing mainly mangoes and avocados."

"Yes, those are the main things being produced around here. I've had a few surfboard lessons, but I would love to learn to do it with a sail. I also love art; I'll pass by sometimes to see your paintings. What would you like to take with you today?"

"That's a nice way to do business," I said, as I took in the scent of freshly baked apple-pies being hauled out of the wood-burning oven.

"Well it's all done like that here, and we all love it. I

remember how running my bakery in Spain had been so stressful that I hardly ever found time to do anything else. I have my girlfriend here with me, and she's a hairdresser. However, you guys don't seem to be looking for a haircut," he laughed. "But she's a great cook, and vegetable paella is her specialty. We'll invite you over sometime."

"It was a pleasure to get to know you, Pepe. And nice doing business with you," we laughed.

We left his shop with fresh bread, croissants and for each of us a piece of cake in hand. We were so elated about the business model in this *world*, as it made each of us feel we had something of value to contribute. We were also glad to have made our first friend here, in our new community.

At the close of my first day in *Freeland*, I decided that I wanted to keep track of how long I'd be here. Therefore, after each sunset, I'd draw a line on a piece of paper.

Chapter 12: Discovering paradise

D uring our first week, we invested a couple of days into garden work, as some chores needed to be done right away, including picking some ripe fruit. We had taken a close look at the gardening journal, and one of our neighbours came over, assessing what needed to be done most urgently and showing us how to do it.

A few days after our first harvest, we went to the local village market. This open market ran something like this: We lay our products out on one of the free tables, and while I stayed at the stall, Robbie would go around seeing what we needed, and inform the other producers what we could offer in return. No cash or mathematics were needed to come to an agreement. We traded most of our produce we had brought, in exchange for coffee, rice, other fruit and vegetables we didn't have, as well as for some beer and wine. The village market also provided an opportunity to meet many of our neighbours, with whom we quickly befriended ourselves, and who'd come over to visit us, or us them.

After enjoying a few days of gardening work, Robbie was dying to go explore *Surfer's Paradise*. So, the following morning, I helped him bring his equipment over to the *bus* stop. The *bus* consisted of two horses pulling a wagon. The driver introduced himself as John, who used to be a bus driver in New York.

"I enjoy travelling; that's why I love doing this," he explained. "I've been here for a couple of years now, and I don't ever want to go back. There is nothing worthwhile back there for me."

One more thing that amazed me here was that everyone would start talking about themselves very openly, with no need to try and squeeze information out of people, as everyone seemed very free in the way they communicated.

With his carriage, John moved both goods and people around. There was a schedule posted at the *bus stop*, which said "about every hour". When one *bus* would pull out from 'Central Station' down in the valley on its way up, the one in our village would start heading down. There was a phone there where they could call each other before leaving. I would still need to find out what "about every hour" meant here. I guess it indicated that if you missed one, you wouldn't need to wait extremely long for the next one.

The small cafeteria right next to the bus stop was managed by an elderly lady from France. She offered fresh croissants she had obtained from the bakery, making it very pleasant to have to wait for a carriage. She had also set up some shelves. "Free library", it read. One could read a book while waiting for the next departure.

John explained to us that from *Central Station* down in the valley, one could catch a ride to wherever he wanted to go on the island. It also hosted the biggest market, where larger amounts of produce were exchanged.

Robbie had taken a few avocados along to pay for his expenses on the trip. "I could use a couple of them," John said. "I'm all for a society where people exchange goods and services, and, most importantly, people are freed to do what they are good at and enjoy, without getting overworked at jobs they don't even like."

Of course, we had never experienced a situation where one needed to take a bag of fruit and vegetables along in exchange for a service or a drink. It was indeed a new and exciting experience for both of us.

"When you embark on a longer trip you should take coffee along," John suggested. "Or, alternatively, some handmade soap. You know; the kind of stuff that doesn't weigh too much in your bag."

Robbie waved goodbye as the carriage started moving downhill. "Thanks for your help Bernardo, I will see you tonight. Have fun!" Robbie was so thrilled about this opportunity to go and catch some waves.

Back at my house I started to mix paint, trying to find those pastel colours I had been experimenting with before leaving Earth, giving my paintings a personal and unique touch. Each angle of the view from my terrace offered a grand view and would be worth painting. The crickets and birds were the only music I listened to while doing my work, and what better music could one have for painting?

It seemed as if my skills improved with every stroke, like some unknown energy was flowing through my hands such as I'd never experienced before. The best part was that it came out just right, without the additional headache of needing to improve anything. The first painting took only about four hours. I knew that because I was still wearing my wristwatch, which continued to work fine here. I finished two paintings that day, and was very pleased with how they both turned out. I'd never done such delicate paintings before, they were truly inspired, and I liked them. I was looking forward to show them to Robbie, and get some feedback from him.

When he arrived back that night, he was in awe about the wonderful waves at the sea and all the other surfers he had met at the beach. "You need to come with me some time, Bernardo. The beach is much longer than the one in *El Medano*, and the waves are just perfect, neither too strong nor too weak. There was a pleasant, steady breeze all day long. Perfect surfing conditions! I met a lot of wonderful people, and I had lunch at a beach bar with palm leaves providing shade, while enjoying a cold beer and food. They were glad I had some avocados, as they had run out. I was able to pay for my lunch and drinks with those."

I don't think I'd ever seen Robbie so excited, like a child who just received a puppy. "Oh, and I met some nice ladies there as well, with whom I exchanged phone numbers. I can't wait to go again. And, you know what the best news is? The surfing school there urgently needs a surfing teacher, as the last one went back to Earth recently." That sure sounded like perfect timing.

Robbie marvelled at my two new paintings. "What has happened to you, Bernardo, you've never painted that good! I like them a lot. And you're really developing your own style now." I was of course very encouraged to hear that.

Time passed by quickly in Freeland. I learned that I needed to find the right balance between social life and solitude. And by solitude, I don't only mean the time I spent painting, but also just sitting still in meditation, or letting my life play out before me, and trying to understand what had happened so far.

I appreciated this time away. It was, as they say, "just what the doctor ordered." Being able to spend a good amount of time dealing with my past, forgiving myself for whatever I felt I might have done wrong and finding peace about it, thus enabling the future to become clearer as well. It was a time of deep reflection over my own life, over what had transpired with Anne, and understanding why it was better that we were no longer together. I still loved her dearly, and would often wonder how she was doing, and how her spiritual life was developing. Deep in my heart I thought that coming to a place like this would possibly do her a lot of good too. But then again, how are we to judge what is good for people or not? It sure was good for me, but that didn't mean that it would be good for everybody, especially if they held on to things on Earth, such as their career or material security.

Robbie had gotten quite busy at the surf-school, and he sometimes would just overnight down there somewhere. He always shared some titbits about the lovely ladies he was teaching to surf. I went a couple times with him, just going for a swim and enjoying the view, having a drink at the beach bar and talking to people.

I was also getting to know lots of new friends right around my house and in the village. We would mainly meet in the evenings, once everyone had done their daily chores. And oh, the interesting people we met, and the trips we took to other regions and valleys, I must tell you about that too.

I wasn't that interested in getting to know new ladies. I was missing Birgit and wondered what she was up to in her life. We had gotten so close, and yet there seemed to be an important hurdle in the way of our getting together. Lately, she was still torn between getting together with Tom, with whom she could start a new family, or a guy like me who already had a family and was trying to sort things out. I could feel that she loved me, but somehow she seemed to still hang on to an idea of how things are *supposed* to be.

It's amazing how traditions, the way things were always done, hinder people from venturing out into something new, I thought to myself. I was of course hoping that, with time, Birgit would be able to choose what her heart told her to do, even if it wasn't the so-called sensible thing to do, or the status quo.

I had many lovely and deep discussions out on the terrace at night, with all kinds of new people from around *Bellezza*. And often, after returning home late at night, I would go back to my canvas and continue working until a painting was completed. The peacefulness and quietness this place offered was a unique opportunity to exercise my newfound passion. A friend from the village had offered to take care of my garden in exchange for a couple of my paintings, which freed me to focus on my work.

One morning, after a young lady had spent the night at his place, Robbie came over for breakfast. He seemed a bit disappointed.

"Naomi left early. Anouk wasn't like that; I have started to miss her over the past couple of weeks. Too bad she isn't here."

"And I miss Birgit, now that I haven't seen her in a while. Nevertheless, I don't want to go back yet, the time is not right for that," I said. "And there is so much I want to still see while here."

"When we're ready to go back we can send a prayer-message to the aliens. I hope they don't have a long waiting-list." We both started laughing.

"Let's go visit a new valley today, maybe the 'Valley of Beer', or whatever it is called."

I chuckled. "It's not the 'Valley of Beer', but the 'Valley of Cereals'." After checking on the map where the place was, we packed some fresh mangoes into a bag and I took a painting with me that I had recently finished.

"Why are you taking a painting along?" Robbie questioned. "Well, I don't even know myself why. I just heard this small voice inside my head, suggesting I should take it with me."

One hour later, we were sitting up on the carriage, making our way down the hill. 'Central Station' was probably the only place in *Freeland* that one could consider busy. Carriages would arrive from every direction, while others were leaving, and the big market next to it was like a beehive, with people loading and unloading goods, while others were busy trading.

"It seems like some people are the kind that need to keep themselves very active, and they seem very pleased with this opportunity to trade around, even though there is no financial benefit involved."

"That's right, Bernardo. Not everyone enjoys a very peaceful pace like we do. Others like to keep themselves more occupied. There seems to be a place for everyone here."

We found the *bus stop* with the sign "Valley of Cereals". The carriage was about to leave, so we hopped on, leaving a few mangoes for the driver. It was a rather long trip, taking a good hour to get up the hills, through villages, and on to the top.

"Look, *Bellezza* is over there on the other side." We could even see the two small spots where we estimated our houses to be.

After arriving on top of the hill, the carriage continued its way through rolling hills, and then entered a long valley saturated with fields of wheat, rye, oats, barley, soy, hops and malt, as the carriage-driver explained to us. We were watching people working in those fields, and, in the absence of heavy duty machinery, they seemed to use simple handmade tools to do the harvesting. Many of them would stop and greet us while passing by.

We were told that this was the valley where most of the cereals used on the island came from. People living in this area were agricultural fanatics, having gathered experience doing the same on Earth, mainly as farmers. Except here they didn't need to work long hours; just enough to trade for other goods which they themselves needed.

"There is no pressure here, as life is so simple that no one needs to keep up with any race for material things. By the way, my name is Henry. I used to be a private driver for some rich people in New Delhi."

We introduced ourselves. It was nice to be able to converse with the drivers here, as there wasn't any type of heavy traffic on the roads that they needed to pay attention to. The roads had space every couple of hundred meters for the carriages to cross each other easily. Henry kept on talking about the industrial revolution. He obviously had a dislike for all the so-called industrial progress and the negative effects it had brought to his country as well.

"When you see people rushing around, stressed out by this industrial revolution, not looking at each other, much less having the time to do so, nor for listening to an aching heart next to them. Then you begin to wonder if weren't better to stop all this industrial progress. Why should mankind be a slave to materialism, instead of caring for nature, for the animals and for each other? Humans can fly to the moon, but are unable to use their intelligence to slow down this evil process and live in harmony."

"We certainly agree with you, Henry. I guess that's one of the reasons why we all have been transferred here: because we prefer a simple and non-materialistic lifestyle."

"That's right, Bernardo, and it's so nice that they don't bring any greedy and materialistic people here."

The people in this valley lived in wooden cottages. However, in addition to their houses, there were also storage-facilities everywhere for the various cereals that were being harvested. There were several mills throughout the valley, so that the harvests didn't need to be brought very far for processing.

"I wonder on what energy these mills are all operated. Would you know?"

"Well, you might have heard about the 'Valley of Energy'. That's where the electricity for the whole island is produced," Henry explained.

"Yes, we've seen it on the map, but we haven't visited yet."

"It's full of windmills. The aliens preferred the windmills all in one place, and the birds know it's a danger zone for them. I think it's better for birdlife that windmills aren't scattered all around the island, perhaps that way they can feel safer."

"That makes sense," said Robbie. "And how the energy is transported to all the houses on the island would be interesting to know too, because I don't see any cables."

"The energy is being distributed to the villages through underground cables, and from there to every house," Henry explained.

"Great idea. All these power cables hanging everywhere on Earth look ugly," Robbie noted. "Do you know if anyone ever sailed away from here to look for other such islands?"

"I haven't heard of anyone having done that until now. I don't think the aliens have explicitly forbidden it. But, perhaps people feel so satisfied to have arrived at such an amazing place that they don't feel the need to go to discover new worlds. But yes, it would be interesting to know if there are other such islands out there."

"I think there probably are," Robbie speculated. "But, even though I enjoy surfing and sailing, I don't presently feel the need to go out to sea in search of other islands. I would much rather go and see my girl again, when I leave this place." I realized at that moment that dear Robbie was missing Anouk much more than I had previously anticipated.

We drove by the brewery, but didn't stop, as we had decided we'd visit it on the way back to pick up some beer.

"If you guys would like to, you could get off at the final

stop at the end of the valley, and take one of the paths back through the hills. I'm fascinated by all the efficient hiking trails that the aliens have set up throughout the island. You've probably seen them on the map. There are fountains all along, and some people have set up inns serving refreshments. You can even find uninhabited cabins in case you might get surprised by the dark or by rainy weather, all fully equipped with beds." *That's awesome*, I thought.

"I've been here for about six months now," Henry continued. "I'm torn between staying and going back. I miss my two kids back in India. But I can see how much I needed this time away from Earth; it's doing me so much good. I feel like all the burdens I was carrying down there have vanished, and I'm finally able to fully live. Maybe at a later point, I might feel ready to go back, but I need to come up with a plan on how I will preserve the peace and tranquillity I've found here. You know?"

"Yes, that makes sense. There is no use going back and getting involved in the same rat-race one was stuck in before coming here, that's for sure."

"That's exactly how I feel, Bernardo. I've been using my time to think about how I would do it, and there have been some concrete plans evolving in my head, which seem to take on shape with each passing day. This is no strenuous occupation I have here; it leaves me with lots of time to think."

"And what are your plans all about, if I may ask?"

"Well, when I get back to Earth, I want to quit my job as a taxi driver for the rich. I've saved up all my tips throughout the years, as I always felt like I might need that money at some point in the future. I would like to get a lodge up in the mountains of northern India: The kind of place where hikers can stay overnight and where I might become a guide, taking people around. I've done so many hikes here, it has become my passion. Of course, there is a certain risk involved, but I'm going to do it anyway. The conviction in my heart has been growing daily, and so has the courage to do something new. Maybe it won't even work out."

"Yes, but what if it will? It's a great plan!" As we got off the carriage, I decided on the spur of the moment to give my painting to Henry. "It's for you, my friend. I call it *The Lonely Traveller.*" He started crying when he saw it.

"I don't think I've ever seen such a divine painting. And look, the crystal is shining in the dark as he looks over that gorgeous valley." He was so touched by it, and so was I. "I hope the aliens will allow me to take it back to Earth when I leave," he said with a hopeful look on his face. "It would forever help me to reach for the stars, and my dreams."

"Your dreams are already manifested in you, Henry. I'm sure you will reach your goals, if you take all the energy you now gain back with you when you leave."

"I could never afford to buy a decent painting before, so this will be the first one hanging on my wall. You guys are so sweet. I hope to see you again, before any of us leave this place."

We exchanged phone numbers, and, with warm goodbyes, were on our way.

Chapter 13: The mystical valley

There were several wooden signs pointing in different directions. "Main trail to the brewery", read one. And, right underneath, but much smaller, was a sign which said: "Mystical valley trail to the brewery." That one caught our attention. There were also many connecting trails to other valleys, and to the tops of some summits to the left. It seemed to truly be a hiker's paradise, just as Henry had mentioned.

After a soft uphill climb, we arrived to the top of the 'Valley of Wheat', and were confronted with a gorgeous view over the whole valley. The various fields that had been planted looked very naturally embedded. We noticed another sign to 'Mystical valley.' Of course, we didn't look at *mystical* as something dark and foreboding, but rather as some secrets worth discovering. We arrived at a place from which we could now see that valley before us. It was very lush, full of endless low trees, overgrown with moss. Clouds of fog would speedily gather, roam around this valley, and then disappear again as quickly as they had appeared.

"Laurels," Robbie pointed out, as we passed by the first trees.

Nature seemed totally undisturbed here, and we could hear numerous birds chirping, as our path led into the rainforest. There was no fear in this peaceful environment, and it seemed clear to us that no animal would harm us so long as we didn't behave in threatening ways. We noticed extremely colourful birds sitting on a branch, while big lizards worshipped the sun on the rocks. Some plants had flowers, whose exotic scents filled the air, as they exploded with intense colours such as I had never seen before. The intensity of the scene was magnified by the flow of immense positive and peaceful energy emerging from each tree, plant, and flower. It was as if each had a life and a soul of its own, emitting its own energy, merging into a consortium of very warm and pleasant light.

"This is amazing!" Robbie exclaimed. "How bright everything is with such intense colours, and I'm not even stoned!"

I was reminded of something I had realized a while back down on Earth: Nature is not only what we see, feel, and hear when being surrounded by it, but there is an energy behind, a positive flow of very good, pure, and loving vibes. And maybe the purpose of this valley was to show this spiritual energy, without any mind-enhancement through drugs or other means. All our fears of the wild, which had been implanted in us since childhood, had vanished, and were replaced by feelings of wonder and magic.

"The perception of magic starts when we hear sounds and feel things we can't explain, which go beyond our usual perception. Most of our magical experiences date back to our childhood, when so much of what we experienced was new, and seemed mystical. Yet, there is still so much of this mystical world left to explore once we start on a spiritual journey."

"That's right Bernardo. I think this experience will deepen my relationship with nature. This place is so pure, holy, and unspoiled. The energy it emits is so strong and loving!"

"It's sad in a way," I continued, "that we need to come to a place like this to recognize what nature really means. Perhaps the last time we felt like this was as children, but then the stress of life set in, and took over those sensations of mystical discovery."

Nature was in full control here, and I wanted to capture every image, registering in my senses all these mystical feelings. I hoped to take them home so I could paint them. I felt that there were a thousand impressions to be painted from this valley alone. Clouds of fog kept moving in from nowhere, keeping this place lush and green. I would have liked to take photographs. It seemed obvious that the aliens didn't want us to take pictures, as I hadn't seen any cameras thus far.

Therefore, I had to awaken my inner perception when going places, and experience moments like these with great intensity, recording the pictures in my mind.

In the middle of the rainforest, the trees suddenly gave way to a big open meadow, with a cosy wooden cottage at the far end. We were very intrigued by this place. Imagine a big round open field of grass in the middle of a rainforest. We walked over to the cottage, which had various animals around, like sheep, goats, a couple horses and some cows. "Bruno and Emily's Inn", stood above the door.

We met Emily and Bruno from Holland. They explained that this was a favourite valley of many people who found it. "We live like hermits here."

"Why is that?" I wanted to know.

Emily explained: "The aliens haven't advertised this place, and it's not even on the map. Therefore, not so many people pass by. It's somewhat hidden and hard to find."

"Well, then we can be even more glad that we found it. We really like it too!"

"Yes, so do we," Emily continued. "We both wanted to get away from people, and that's what got us here," she smiled. "The people passing by offer enough socialization for us, and we have all these animals around. They already were here when we arrived, and have never left. They love to interact with us. Maybe it's because they know we are animal lovers; they can feel that. There isn't an animal that doesn't appreciate us looking at them lovingly, and with no intention of killing them, nor doing them harm."

I noticed a few hens running around the backyard, while a lovely Swiss mountain dog came to greet us. "He's the dog we had in Holland. We are so lucky that Benjamin was transferred too!" Emily explained.

They invited us for some food and drinks. We only had mangoes left, and I had given away my painting. They weren't interested in surfing lessons with Robbie. "Don't worry guys. You seem to be very interesting people to talk to. Just eat and drink all you want."

I turned to Robbie: "You know what this place reminds me of? 'La Laguna Grande'. I'm sure you must have been there as well."

"Now that you say it, I was wondering why this place looked so familiar to me. The rainforest here, and now this place, all look so much like La Gomera."

"We've been there on holiday," the couple explained, "We were so fascinated that time to see Laguna Grande, and this place here does resemble it."

"What is this big round patch of grass in the middle of the rainforest all about?" Robbie wanted to know.

"Well, no one knows for sure, but various people have suggested that the aliens landed here when they first came to set up *Freeland*. And then nothing else grew back, except for that wonderful green grass."

"That's amazing, because I've heard similar stories about Laguna Grande," Robbie said. "This must be a very special place to live."

"Yes. Many people mention that they can feel a special aura around here, and we feel very blessed to be here, and so do the animals."

"You know, we've had lots of time to think about our lives while here. We would like to stay, but the only reason we consider going back would be to share our thoughts with others. We have been granted so many wonderful impressions here, and they are so needed down there."

"They sure are," Robbie agreed. "Heaven on Earth is what we see here in this purest form of nature, the animals, and kind hearts such as yours. Whereas hell on Earth is all the suffering, selfishness, destruction, and pain brought on by mankind. It's difficult to coexist with both, because even when you manage to create your own bit of heaven down there, you are still faced, almost daily, with all the evil going on."

"Yes," Emily sighed. "That's why we've been hesitant to return. Nonetheless, the world needs to hear about this ideology, even though we may not talk about *Freeland* itself."

"We've gotten so close to the animals here in this valley.

I've even learned to communicate with them and am able to see their whole lives in their eyes," she said, with a sort of questioning look, hoping we'd understand. This reminded me of my experience I'd had with that deer after I'd been transferred.

"Oh yes, Emily. I've had a similar experience with a deer. But that time I was on my way to the gathering and didn't have time to get fully into it. So, it is true, I felt that one might be able to communicate with the animals here in some way."

"It is, Bernardo, and one can truly learn to interact with them from soul to soul. We're thinking of opening an animal centre for abandoned animals once we get back. The thought of doing that fills us with so much joy. But it's also hard to leave this place, and, as Emily said, we don't feel quite ready yet," Bruno explained.

"Neither do we," Robbie replied, while looking over at me to see if I agreed.

"I guess it's better to go back when one feels filled up with enough new energy, and a renewed and clear vision of what they plan on doing back there. Otherwise one might want to come right back," I suggested.

"There is something to that, Bernardo. We aren't planning on going back and forth; it's not our thing. That's why we are waiting for the right moment, when we both feel ready to return."

Robbie was still thinking about the possibility that the aliens had landed here when they came to the island.

"Maybe the first thing they did after landing was to open that brewery nearby." We all had a good laugh over Robbie's speculation.

"Anyway, that's where we're heading now. Thanks so much to both of you for your sweet hospitality. If you want, I can send a painting this way with the local mail system."

"Oh, that would be so lovely, Bernardo. Could you do one of this place; with our cottage on it? Maybe the aliens would allow for it to be sent back with us to Holland when we leave."

It was so cute how everyone hoped so much that some of

their *souvenirs* from this place would get transferred along with them when they left. Bruno brought a small bag with herbs and gave it to Robbie. I guess somehow he knew that Robbie used that stuff more than I did.

"I call it 'Bruno's Special.' It grows wild here."

"Oh, really?" Robbie rejoiced.

"Well, not along the path you took; but I know where," he said with a twinkle in his eye.

The trip to the brewery was not very long, as the largest part of the trail was already behind us. Our path led again through the rainforest. We eventually came out of the valley, and there stood the brewery. We were both looking forward to a cold beer. Johannes, a German brewer, was there to receive us and to show us around before offering us a seat. We put our last couple of mangoes down on the table.

"We produce three kinds of beer here: blond, dark, and the 'Freeland Special'. Which one would you like to try?" We went for the last one he mentioned, as we hadn't tried that one before. It was ice-cold and fabulous. "I've been here for a couple of months, and I'm so glad I landed here, after working in a German brewery. I would have missed my work too much. My dream is to open my own beer-garden somewhere, and brew my very own beer." He was passionate about it. I wondered why he was here, but didn't need to wait long for an answer to that.

"I don't enjoy working in big companies. I would like to have more time to interact with people, instead of being so involved in production. When my wife died of cancer, it was a very difficult time for me, and I started searching for answers. I guess that's why I somehow ended up here. It's very good for me, having time to sort out what I'd like to do with my life, including making clear plans on how to achieve my goals once I'll go back. Any day now, someone else might be serving you beer here," he smiled.

"What? Did you send in your request for transfer?" we inquired.

"Yes, last night. And I am not worried. Everyone I know

who sent a request was transferred within a couple of days. The aliens have never failed."

"That certainly puts us at ease. Although right now we're still very much enjoying ourselves here, with many more places we'd like to visit, and with no urgency to go back."

"You will feel it when the time is ready. It's hard to explain."

"Well, have a good transfer. And great success with your goals and dreams, Johannes," we wished him, as we said farewell.

Robbie and I ended up catching what seemed to be the last carriage down that day, this time with another driver. We enjoyed the relaxing trip downhill, as the sun set over the *ocean*. We were very grateful for this magic day we'd had, and although we hadn't done that much, the intensity of what we had experienced had been very impressive. While going off to sleep that night, I had thousands of pictures filling my mind that I desired to paint.

Chapter 14: Days of Heaven

For the first time, I started thinking about my own transfer. I missed Birgit and Jasi. At the same time, I wanted to paint as many of these impressions as possible, as I just wasn't sure how much I'd remember when I would get back home. I also wanted to visit some other valleys, and that's what we did over the next weeks.

The 'Valley of Cacti' was certainly one of my favourites. It seemed more like a theme park in some ways, as little pathways made their way around the valley, so that one could go around and see all the thousands of wonders from as close as possible. At the entrance to 'Cacti Paradise', as it was called, there was a *shop* where you could get cacti *babies* to take back with you. We met some very lovely people working there with the plants, who seemed to fully enjoy what they were doing.

Another trip led us to the 'Freeland Alps', the highest mountain range on the island. We took warm clothing with us, as we were told that it can get quite chilly, mainly because of the massive glacier up there. On the path leading up, I discovered all the alpine flowers and trees that I knew from my youth: Gentian, edelweiss, thistles, soldanella, snow bells, buttercups. crocus, and many more. Yes, you probably noticed: All the spring, summer and autumn flowers were out at the same time! And there were herbs of all kinds, some of which we picked up to take home, such as wild mint, thyme, rosemary, which I could still remember from my hikes with my dad.

We came upon a couple of mountain lakes with 'Swiss stone pine' and 'Scots pine' around, and sat down overlooking one of them while having our lunch. It was fed by sparkling mountain streams flowing down from all sides.

Someone had built a stone tower on top of the summit, which was right above the magnificent and only glacier on this island. For sure there wasn't going to be any global warming here, and no risk for this beauty to start melting away.

We sat down to enjoy this outstanding scene. I had seen glaciers before, but this one shone in some very mystical blue-greenish light, like a mix of emerald and turquoise. "Wow! I wonder if I might be able to find the right mix for these colours, that would be fantastic!" We both were totally stunned by what we saw. We couldn't see how far the ice went as it took a curve around some mountain, but the peaks and cliffs all around, with patches of snow on them, offered a terrific panorama. Not only that, but behind us we could see the hills and valleys rolling out towards the ocean in the far distance. But, unlike as had been the case from on top of Mount Teide, we couldn't see any other islands on the horizon.

Since this was our major and longest trip, taking several hours to hike up, we ended up having to spend the night at a small refuge on our way down. It was already dark when we got there, and we were glad we had taken the crystals with us, which we were both carrying to give light on this rocky path. After passing some wild mountain goats, we found our abode for the night. The wooden hut was fully equipped with beds and a wood stove, with a few candles to offer light, and even some food which someone must have left there. We wrote our names into the guest-book, and spent some time reading the various comments and poems other hikers from around the world had put there. The general tenor in that book was that people had never seen as amazing a view as this glacier offered. Someone had written: "Make sure you get up on time for the sunrise! You wouldn't want to miss that."

The sun rose early the next day, and what a spectacle that was. There was a coffee-maker, and we made ourselves some fresh coffee on the stove. We had been adding some wood to the fire every now and then, and were thankful for whoever had carried the old branches here. We were watching the sunrise with our mug in hand. Words would fail to describe the energy that we could feel flowing through body and soul, as we were watching the sun rise over the hills. We went in search of some wood to replace what we had used, leaving the rest of our provisions for future *lonely travellers* who would find their way there.

During the following weeks, I got very involved with painting. I finished several paintings of the glacier, seen from different angles, as the excursion there had left lasting impressions on me. I felt satisfied with the way I managed to mix the colours and find the right tones to reflect what I'd experienced there.

During that time, Robbie was travelling some more, and he also returned to see Emily and Bruno's cottage, taking along the painting I had made for them. He was interested to learn more from them about communicating with animals, as he was hoping to get a dog in the future, and perhaps some other animals too. And maybe he was looking forward to receive some more of Bruno's herbs as well. He called me the first evening he was there, letting me know that it was so interesting that he would be staying a few days with them, as learning to communicate with the animals was not only very fascinating, but it also required some time.

He explained that usually one needed to be around an animal for a couple of days before they'd be ready to offer you a glimpse of their soul. Since they had all been transferred there from the world, they were still quite shy and sceptical of humans they didn't know. Many of them had been affected by some dreadful experiences. But once you gained their trust they would come over to communicate, and that would be an "incredible trip", as Robbie put it. Emily had explained to him that this wasn't a result of special powers we were given while here, but due to being more spiritually sensitive; more focused spiritually, and not side-tracked by all the confusion of the world.

When Robbie got back he seemed like another person. "This has been the most amazing experience of my life! One of the horses took a special liking to me, and just this morning,

'Storm', as he's called, came over and stared at me. I caressed him and felt a flow of energy coming from his head through my hand. At the same time, it I was like being sucked into his eyes and I started seeing sequences from his younger years. The owners had been training him to become a racehorse, but there were scenes I couldn't watch. It hurt too much; he wasn't treated with love. I was so glad that he ended up being transferred here, where he has experienced peace and is well taken care of. At the same time, I think he also got a glimpse of my life as a human, and it seemed interesting enough for him too, as he kept watching. I hope you'll get to experience that too." He started crying while telling me that.

"Wow, Robbie! That's indeed an unforgettable happening. I imagine that since the animals being brought here might have all experienced some horror before being transferred here, I am not so interested in watching that. You know me. I'm a bit sensitive for that kind of stuff. But it's good that some people can stand it, and realize the pain and agony they have gone through." I remembered some animal activists trying to show me an album with photos about the way animals were mistreated for tests, and I needed to look away. The activists didn't mean harm, as they were just trying to show people the realities of animals being abused. I hope more mistreated animals and people will be brought here to get a rest from the cruelty on Earth."

Robbie agreed: "Maybe with time they will. At least the aliens have started some type of intervention now. If they were to intervene more fully they'd upset the free choice people have. It's a very controversial topic, and I'm sure glad I'm not the one who has to make such decisions."

"Yes, it's a sad story that so many have to suffer for the bad choices others make."

The day after coming back, Robbie stepped out of his bedroom on the terrace, and said with sleepy eyes. "I think we've soon seen just about everything that there is to see, and I feel like I'm now so filled up with all these experiences that I fear my head will explode. I was hungry for this place, but now that I've been fed so abundantly, I feel like there is so much I need to go and share."

"Yes. I feel like I'm getting ready too, and I'm glad you bring this up. Perhaps it's soon time for us to seriously get together and ask for our transfer."

"I think I am ready. I now know very clearly what I want and need to do. That is to get together with Anouk if she desires the same, and hopefully she'll move in with me. She had mentioned that possibility before, and had even offered to move to Tenerife, but I wasn't ready for it at the time. And, as I've already mentioned, I would like to move up to where you are, in hopes of being able to do some serious gardening, and start growing my own stuff. And have some animals to be good to!" This time here had obviously been a life changer for him too.

"I have a couple of paintings to finalize that are nearly done. Maybe we can get together in a couple of days and send in our *reservations* for our *flight*," I suggested, which, of course, made us both laugh again. It sounded quite funny.

"Yes! Oversized luggage included," Robbie added. We both realized how extremely lucky we could count ourselves for having had this free holiday in this unforgettable place.

"Do you realize that although we've been here for a couple of months, our bills at home won't have added up? They'll be the same as if we had never left."

"That's wonderful, Bernardo! I haven't thought about that. And usually, after coming back from such a long holiday, the mailbox is full of bills that need to be paid. On top of it, my flat won't be any dirtier either."

"Yes. We've lived for free during this time, with no bills and taxes. It will be hard to think back on all the lovely people we've met here, the peaceful and unselfish interaction this place offers, as well as the harmonious interaction between nature and the inhabitants. But now my heart is aching to go back too."

"Do you think when we die we'll be going to a similar place to the one here?"

"That would have been a good question to ask the aliens. One of the people I've met in the village asked them that, and they said something to the effect that it's not for us to know; but that we won't be disappointed."

"That makes sense. I mean, why would they have allowed us to come here to experience this wonderful place, and situation, if we'd go to some crappy place when we die?" Robbie reasoned.

"Maybe *Freeland* is like a little taste of what our future home might be like. At least that's what I suspect, or perhaps wish for."

"I think so too. And, it can be speculated that the same aliens that brought us here might have something to do with our transfer in the future, when we die."

"I wouldn't mind to meet them again, really. They were lovely people."

"Anyways, Bernardo, having been here has done me a lot of good. I see a lot clearer now what I want to do with my life back home. I think we can be a positive influence when we go back, and perhaps we can change some things."

"Well, yes and no. There are a lot of evil powers in the world. I don't think we'll be able to change those. The idea that any one of us might be able to change the world seems like wishful thinking to me. It's like a tree that has grown the wrong way, which can't be bent back to normal without breaking it."

"You're right, my friend. Some direct intervention by the aliens seems inevitable in the future, and perhaps one day they will invade the world and set up *Freeland* down there," Robbie suggested.

"Perhaps; but, then they could have done that already, and stopped all the suffering and destruction. We don't know why they do what they do. They seemed very loving to me, so there must be a good reason why they haven't yet invaded planet Earth. Maybe that would interfere too much with the free will humanity has been used to. Maybe instead of going there like new dictators, they prefer to bring some of the people and animals here, like they did with us."

"Free will that is so often used by humanity for evil, that's for sure. But I don't want to question the goodness of our hosts. They've been extremely kind to us in letting us spend this time here. I certainly feel very obliged to them," Robbie continued. "But I just can't believe that all this evil will forever continue in the world without there ever being a stop to it. Nor do I want to think that wars and the destruction of the environment can go on without there ever being some consequence for the perpetrators."

I guess he expressed what many of us felt. If there are species or powers above humanity, then they might want to start acting as some sort of police soon, or how much evil would there need to happen before a cup is full?

"If they were to enforce the *no greed* rule, as is being done here, it might even be acceptable for most humans. But some would surely make a big fuss against it, and might cause even more wars on earth to keep themselves in power."

"I feel so too, Bernardo. Perhaps the aliens are testing here to see how it goes. Well, as far as I'm concerned it goes very well. But I doubt that this would work as smoothly in the materialistic world, with so many greedy people hanging around there," Robbie concluded.

Over the next days, I finished up my two paintings, while Robbie went down for a couple of days to the beach, saying his goodbyes to everyone he knew there. I went around the village, talking to various friends once more, and exchanging addresses to retain our friendships once back on Earth. Then, when the evening arrived, we purposely didn't invite anyone over, as we wanted to both concentrate on communicating our request to the aliens. We took it very seriously, and felt we needed to focus and send a strong and clear message to our hosts, in hopes that they'd understand that we meant business, and would want to go back now for good.

"You do this, Bernardo; you are better at prayers."

So, with both of us sitting there, sort of bowing our heads, I began muttering a prayer: "Dear God; dear universe; dear angels and aliens. Both Robbie and I have greatly benefitted from our time here, and would like to express our deepest gratitude for having had the privilege to come and enjoy this wonderful place freely, and at your expense and kindness. Thank you!"

I saw Robbie nodding his head, and I continued: "We both feel that our time to return has come. We've taken in as much as we feel capable of, and we now miss our loved ones, and would like to share all the joy, and good vibes that we have experienced here, with them. So please feel free to transfer us in the easiest way and as quickly as possible."

Robbie added: "Agreed", which he probably meant as something like the Christian term *amen.* We didn't laugh this time, but looked at each other in silence, wondering when the transfer was going to happen.

"You're still here, Bernardo," Robbie joked and looked at me. "We need to lighten up, and just go with the flow. We're still here, so we might as well smoke a pipe."

He had gotten himself the most intricate wooden pipe, which someone had handcrafted in the 'Valley of Carpentry'. He filled it with herbs from the bag that Bruno and Emily had given him on his last visit. We conversed for a while longer, before going to bed and dozing off into a peaceful sleep. *This has been the best time of my life*, was my last thought.

Chapter 15: Back to the future

I had a very lovely dream, in which I was running down some meadows towards a little cottage, from which I could see Birgit waving at me. *Once more one of those kinds of dreams where one prefers not to wake up.* But I apparently did wake up and saw the sky illuminated with stars and the full moon above me. I sat up and immediately realized that I was no longer in my bed, and when I saw all the lava rocks around me, I knew I had been transferred back to Mount Teide. I wasn't sad about it.

There was a feeling of relief, as well as one of anticipation about the new prospects in my life. I surveyed my surroundings, and found the two girls and Robbie still sleeping next to me. I don't know what woke him up, but suddenly he sat upright in his sleeping back and looked at me.

I pointed to my lips, signalling to him that we should be quiet. We both communicated with our eyes and smiles, glad that our trip back had gone so smoothly. We couldn't sleep anymore; we were too excited for that. We walked some distance away from the girls, so that they wouldn't hear us if they'd wake up.

"We made it, Bernardo! This is wonderfully weird! The girls are still sleeping. I wonder how much they actually know."

"I don't think they know anything besides those lights dancing around the moon, but we'll see. I am glad we made it safely back and I am looking forward to talk to Jasi and to see Birgit again. At the same time, I have mixed feelings about going back to my life. Maybe we'll just get sucked back into the former daily routine. I sure hope this experience won't wear off quickly in the humdrum of day-to-day life on Earth. It won't be easy."

"Yes. We must draw on that experience, and keep it alive in our hearts. I know that we won't experience the same amount and intensity of positive vibes and good energy we'd gotten accustomed to over the past two months. And we will again be faced with the daily battle of trying to earn a living and make ends meet."

"That was an incredible journey! I wonder if anyone would believe us if we told them. But, of course, we won't, and can't. It's certainly much better like that."

We refreshed ourselves with some of the drinks and food that were still left in our bags, which were just the way we had left them when our *friends* had come to take us away.

"I wonder if all of our stuff will have been shipped back to our homes; like your surfboard, my paintings, and other things."

"So do I. Quite a few aliens must have been very busy all night, getting us and our stuff back here."

Both of us were quite eager to return home, so as soon as the girls woke up we told them that we'd like to go back down to the valley for some coffee. The girls didn't mind. They were still very excited about the "dancing of the stars around the moon", as they called it. They said it was the greatest thing they'd ever seen. We couldn't tell them how much more there was to experience, but we knew they could do so too when they would be ready.

As the gondola was still closed that early in the morning, we decided to hike to the valley, as it would be quicker. The sun had now fully risen, so we could easily see the path leading downhill. We reached my beetle, and drove it back down the winding road towards the sea. At the first village, we happily noticed that the cafeteria was already open, and we sat down and relished a nice coffee with croissants.

After bringing the girls back to their place, I drove Robbie home, and I went up with him to check if our belongings had been transferred. Everything was there, even his recently acquired wooden pipe. We then drove up to my house, only to find that everything had been moved there as well, including all my new paintings that I'd done while in *Freeland*. I was very relieved, because I'd done hours and hours of work on them.

I decided to go to work in the afternoon and called the company to let them know I'd be in later. We were relaxing on my terrace, having some lunch, when Anne called.

"Bernardo, where have you been? I've tried to call a few times over the weekend." I told her about our excursion to see the full moon up on Mount Teide. "I've read all about it in the papers, people have seen lights jumping up and down around the moon."

"Really? In the news?"

"Yes. It said that quite a few people saw them, and there was even a hazy photo published, but the paper said that it was probably 'fake'."

"Anyways, I wanted to let you know that Jasi called yesterday. She will be coming to visit next weekend, so I was wondering if we could do something together." That sounded great. It was nice to hear Anne being so jolly and upbeat. Gone were the times when I harboured ill feelings towards her and the way our relationship, and family, had broken apart.

After siesta, I went to my office and the afternoon passed by quickly. It was amazing to think that I had been away for two months, but here I was back at the same moment in time in which I had left. *Strange things do happen*, I thought.

After getting home that night, I called Jasi: "Sorry for calling so late, my baby."

"What happened to you? Mom told me everything about your trip to the mountain, and the news in the papers about lights around the moon. I had told you that something would happen, I felt it. Are you ok?"

"I'm just fine! I had a wonderful experience watching the full moon up there with my friends, and I will tell you all about it when you come to visit for the weekend. I also have some new paintings which I want you to see."

"New ones? In such a short time since I was last there?"

"Yes, Jasi, I've been working hard," I said, truthfully. My whole collection was there: fifteen new paintings. I must have had an extra portion of creativity while away. The colours were so full and deep that I didn't know if I would be able to get such wonderful mixes again.

"I called Mom yesterday as I decided to come next weekend. It's just that after our last talk on the phone I was still a bit worried and decided to come and see if you're all ok. Lolita will be coming with me as well."

Lolita was her friend and roommate. I'd never met her and was looking forward to get to know her.

It was time to call Birgit. She hadn't heard about the lights at full moon, but was very interested to hear more. I told her about everything that had happened on our trip to the summit, except about the transfer and my absence. "I missed you," I added.

"What, just over the weekend? You know I'm always here for you; you're my best friend!" If she only knew that I hadn't seen her for two months. I wondered if she were away for that long, if she'd miss me too? We agreed that she'd be coming to my house the next evening to see my new paintings.

"Where is this place, Bernardo?" Birgit asked, as she studied my 'Freeland collection'. "Wow, you've been painting a lot lately. What happened to you? And these places you painted seem to be so magical. I wonder if such places only exist in your mind, or if they do for real? It looks so peaceful and harmonious. The people on there seem to live at peace with each other and with themselves."

She sighed: "I would like to be at peace with myself too, but I haven't been lately. Are you, Bernardo?"

"Well, I feel a lot more so than a while back, that's for sure. I used to be much more in disharmony with myself, as you know, wondering what this life is all about."

"Yes, Bernardo, you seem less restless, as if you have found some inner peace. How did that happen so quickly?"

"I guess it was the experience up on Mount Teide, along with my newfound passion in painting," which was the truth, or at least part of it. I mentioned it casually, avoiding further details about the full moon experience. "I felt quite ready to find some answers, and the universe responded. Sort of like receiving answers to prayers, I guess."

"You seem a little reluctant to talk about it; I understand. I guess everyone needs to make spiritual experiences on their own. It's a very personal thing that one doesn't feel like advertising to the whole world, as some of the effect may get lost that way."

"That's exactly the way it is," I answered, somewhat relieved that she stopped pressing for details.

"Maybe if I continue to look and pray sincerely for answers, I will also find them."

"Of course you will. Everyone can, if they want to. It was you who got me into praying more again, remember? Now you might want to try it yourself."

I felt so much for her, and knew that it was up to her to reach out. I was sure that the aliens would want to grant her that wish as well. In some way, I felt she would be much more deserving of visiting *Freeland* than I was. Since last time I saw her, she seemed more desperate and ready to reach out for the unknown.

I had finished the first painting for Tom, and asked her if she could bring it to him. "Of course I will; he's been asking about it ever since!"

I still felt some heartache whenever I was with her and his name came up, but I certainly was more peaceful about it now than before my time away. I became aware of how much faith I had gained, trusting for things to work out as they are meant to, and how much I had needed that experience with all these positive effects it had on my life.

When Jasi visited the following weekend, she brought her friend, Lolita, along, and they totally fell in love with my 'Freeland collection', wanting to take all my paintings back with them. "We are going to open a gallery; we absolutely want all of your paintings to be there!"

We revelled in a lovely weekend together. Anne and Mat came over for dinner, which Jasi and Lolita had prepared. The next day we went to *El Medano*, where Robbie gave the girls their first lesson in windsurfing, while Anne, Mat and I sat down for a drink.

The girls spent Monday morning wrapping up all my paintings to get them ready to take with them back to Madrid, and I then drove them to the airport. "Do you and Birgit love each other?" she asked me, while Lolita had gone to make a phone call. I had some explaining to do, so I told her that the feelings didn't seem to be mutual, but that it could still go either way. "I think you both match really well. I will pray that things will work out for you." I was surprised to hear that.

"That's sweet of you! You pray too?"

"I have started recently. Like when I had that strange feeling when you went up to Mount Teide, I prayed that you'd be safe, and that's what happened."

Pablo gave me his permission to hang up my new paintings in the office, as he thought it would be an additional magnet to draw people in, so I could sell more excursion tickets. Buyers ranged from elderly expats, to young alternative tourists on their way back from La Gomera. I had put up a sign: "Selling my own paintings", and people would often drop by even if they weren't interested in booking an excursion, but just to see the paintings. What I couldn't sell, Jasi would take with her on her next visit.

It made my job at the office so much more exciting with people coming in and looking at my paintings. "Well, maybe the day will come when you can quit your job and only paint. To me, that would seem like a better use of your time," Jasi used to say on the phone.

"That would be great, Jasi. I'm looking forward to that day too, but right now I still need to work at the office to cover my expenses and to pay back the credit for the house."

A few weeks had passed, when Birgit called me and sounded very excited: "Bernardo, would you come up with us to see the full moon on Mount Teide? My friends from Germany are visiting, and we'll be going together. I want to see it to; it seems to have had such a great effect on you."

148

"It would be nice, but Robbie has already asked me to go surfing with him, and I have been prevented from going so many times before. I think I'd like to go now and try it." She seemed disappointed. "Isn't Tom going with you?" I must have sounded a bit sarcastic.

"No, he isn't. And he's not my shadow, if that's what you're trying to indicate." Our conversation remained friendly enough to wish each other a nice time.

He isn't her shadow, she had said. I needed to think about that one for a while, but since that didn't shed more light on the matter, I decided that maybe some clarifying future talk might do that.

I had a wonderful weekend, with Robbie filling me in on all the do's and don'ts of windsurfing, and teaching me how to best get on and off the board, keep my balance, letting the wind catch my sail, and turning it to change direction. We had so much fun. At the end of the day we lay in the sand, letting ourselves dry by the hot sun.

"Bernardo, is there still something going on between Birgit and you?"

"Ha! Everybody's asking me lately! Well, there has been on my end, as you know. But she has been torn between whether she wants a relationship or not, and who it should be with."

"You mean, she's choosing between you and another guy?"

"Yes, she likes Tom as well. And you know me; I stay out of competitions. That's simply not for me and far too stressful. I'd rather trust that things that should happen will happen. And if not, it's probably better like that. I do love her a lot, but that includes letting her find herself, and what she wants. And, in the meantime, I have certainly not been on a sad trip because of it."

"You certainly haven't," he smiled. "Let's go for some food and drinks, and then enjoy a smoke on my terrace."

Later, as we watched the sunset from his terrace, we got into a discussion about God. "Do you believe in God,

Bernardo? I mean in the religious sense?" Here we knew each other so well, yet that question hadn't even come up yet.

"Well, I don't believe in the old man we were taught to believe in, who sends everyone to hell who breaks religious rules. I do believe there is a loving power or energy that makes sure the planets don't crash, and that sprinkles water on the flowers so that they can grow, and keeps the sun far enough away so they won't get burned. And sends help, like in form of aliens for example."

"That was nicely said. I also don't believe in God in the traditional sense. I believe we are supposed to make our own choices."

"Well, Robbie, I wouldn't pray if I didn't believe in some loving power answering my prayers. I call out in expectation of answers. Jesus said that if we ask we will receive; if we knock it shall be opened to us. And Buddha said that the greatest prayer is patience. Answers don't always come on the spot. And sometimes not in the way we would expect. However, I believe that many prayers are answered with time." I remembered that's what Birgit had said.

"Yes. Maybe not all prayers are answered because some things simply wouldn't be good for us, or for those we're praying for. We may send in a request for help or for certain situations to work out the way we wish. But the request is only granted if it benefits us and others."

"That's very good reasoning! I have been praying for both Birgit and Jasi to be able to see *Freeland* in due time. Maybe it will happen if it's good for them. I will start adding Anne to that prayer too; it would be lovely if she'd be able to take a trip there. I think it would do her a lot of good as well."

"I think that's very kind of you, Bernardo."

"Well, yes, kindness is important. I think it's helped both Anne and I to sail smoother through our separation. It's better to wish each other well, rather than letting ourselves be led by all kinds of negative feelings for each other."

"Yes, I learned that after Anja had left me. We need to wish people well that are no longer a part of our lives. Perhaps they've hurt us or we hurt them, or both. But to wish them well can release negative energy we may be harbouring against them, which would only poison our own soul. And you guys have managed quite well, even though you may have had rough days as well."

"Yes we did, Robbie. I was upset and had bad nights, and we both answered each other unkindly at times. I think that kind people aren't always kind, sometimes they fail. But because kindness is their ideology, they keep trying to be kind, while others have given up long ago."

"That's an excellent point about kindness," he commented. "I noticed that you have never gotten into talking negative about Anne, and I admire that in you. Because even if someone may think that something is wrong with a person, we shouldn't go around talking bad about them. Because there is always something wrong with us as well, especially if we go talking bad about others behind their back. We need to let people find out on their own whether they should like a person or not."

"Anway, I've asked you about your belief in God because I had been praying that Anouk and I would be able to get together, and it looks like my prayers are being answered. We have missed each other very much ever since she went back to Holland. As you know, being away has helped me realize that. We call each other often. By the way, she always sends her love to you, and last time she sent greetings to you from Betje. I will be flying to Amsterdam next week to spend some time with Anouk."

"That's brilliant! I think you guys match well."

"She's the kind of woman I'd like to get a little house with up in the hills. You might not have me moving in with you after all, like we had been discussing."

"I'm very excited for you guys, that sounds great! Betje and I seemed to have more of a holiday adventure. We write each other sometimes, but I think she enjoys her independence, and my heart has clearly fallen for Birgit. That's also something that became quite clear to me while away."

"Well, whatever is meant to be, will be. We need to follow

our hearts, but if doors aren't open for now, we must accept that. We shouldn't try to run into doors that aren't open. That's where the patience comes in that Buddha talked about."

"Yes, that's the way I see it too. There's some truth in every religion. However, I don't think religion is all there is. Spirituality to me is much more important than the religious traditions that have been established. A sincere search can put you in contact with the power of the universe. That to me seems much more important than the keeping of religious traditions."

"I enjoy this conversation, Bernardo. I think since having been to *Freeland*, we are able to converse on a much deeper level."

"Yes, I find that we're opening much more to each other in our communications, and that's really awesome. We've become good friends, and I really appreciate you."

"That's the same from my side. And I believe that we have exciting times ahead of us."

Chapter 16: When dreams come true

At the beginning of the following week, I went to visit Birgit during working hours. It was already evening, and I had closed my office earlier as I wanted to pass by and see her. I had finished the painting I had made for her, the one where she's sitting by *the rocks*, stringing seashells on a necklace. I felt this would be a good time to bring it to her. *One needn't always wait for a birthday or some other special occasion to give someone a gift*, I thought.

"Oh, Bernardo, this is absolutely adorable!" she screamed out, and gave me a big hug and kiss. "I need to find the right place for this. It must have been a lot of work, as it has so many details."

She couldn't stop raving about it, even after she had closed her shop.

"And I must tell you about the weekend!" She was all excited, as we started walking. "We got to see those same lights around the moon which you had seen! It was just like you had described, and I wonder if this is some new phenomenon that occurs regularly now. We've all seen them and it was the most incredible experience. And it had the same effect on me that it had on you: I found a lot of peace that night, with so many things becoming clearer."

"Like what?" I wanted to know.

"Well, regarding my life and what I should do. One thing was that I needed to stop my relationship with Tom, before it went any further. So, after returning from the mountain with the gondola, I didn't drive back with my friends. I drove straight to Puerto to talk to Tom, letting him know how I feel about him and I."

"That's courageous," I acknowledged.

153

"Doing this has taken such a burden off my heart, and I feel so much freer and happier. It was tough for Tom, as he was hoping that our relationship would deepen and that we could even end up starting a family. I felt sorry for him, but still, I knew in my heart that I needed to do this. I believe that the energy and presence of those lights at full moon gave me the power and courage to do so."

"It's definitely not easy to tell someone that your feelings for them aren't what they had expected or hoped for. I wish things will go well for him, he's a nice guy," I said, feeling quite sorry for him.

"Yes, it wasn't easy to tell him, but I'm glad I took that step and I feel much better now and I'm sure he will find his way. We agreed to stay friends. But I won't see him for the time being as we both need to find our distance. And you know what?"

She paused for a minute and I was expectantly looking forward to the rest of the news. "I decided today to go for three weeks to Germany and learn to do the work Tom has been doing for me!"

"Oh really? That's thrilling!" I said, while trying to take in and place all these new events.

We made our way down to *the rocks*, and I felt her snuggling up to me. It felt so warm and familiar. She seemed a lot more relaxed, peaceful and excited about the future than last time I'd seen her.

"I want to learn to do the melting and moulding myself, and I just found a professional jeweller who will take me in to teach me. He's a client of mine who's here on holiday. He and his wife visited my shop today and we started talking about this possibility. They've invited me and even have a room for me. I won't need to pay anything as he needs some additional help and will teach me everything I need to know. I have already acquired some knowledge about making moulds, having observed Tom so many times."

"Are you certain about breaking up with Tom?"

"Yes, I've had time to think about it. My feelings have

been running in a different direction." That was some news.

She was putting her head on my shoulder as we sat on one of our favourite rocks. Then, out of the blue, she turned toward me and, holding my face with both hands, began to kiss me.

"Wow, your feelings are indeed going into a new direction," I gasped.

"I love you Bernardo, I really do. Sorry that it's taken so long to get my feelings, and hurts from the past, sorted out." We kissed and embraced like two teenagers, as the sun set in front of us. People passed us by, and we didn't even notice them. "Bernardo, will you come home with me?"

She put on some soft music, lit a candle and some incense, and started kissing me again. "I missed you, Bernardo; you can't imagine how much."

"I missed you too, but you needed time."

I never thought she'd be so wild. Both of us were finally able to let each other know and feel how much we appreciated and loved each other.

"Don't go, Bernardo," she whispered. "Please stay, and never leave again."

I couldn't figure out what had happened to her. But some things just need to be accepted and enjoyed, without having to be figured out, especially when they feel that good.

I didn't sleep much, and as the first sunrays made their way into the room, I went down to the bakery to get some breakfast. Birgit was sleeping, so I took my time, and went for a walk along the shore.

In these early morning hours, there were only a few fishermen down at the pier, unloading the fish they'd caught that night. The sea was peaceful and calm, just like my feelings were this morning. I tried to sort out in my mind what had happened, but I couldn't figure out what had changed her. When I got back, she still hadn't gotten up, so I made some coffee on the stove.

"Bernardo, do I smell coffee?" I heard her ask from the bed. I brought it to her, along with fresh pastries. I gently kissed her forehead, and she pulled my head down for a deep, long kiss. "That's brilliant, my love. I haven't had breakfast in bed for so long. You're the sweetest man I know and I feel fortunate you stayed with me tonight! I didn't sleep much, but I think I will be very fit today." I was of course very glad she had gotten her feelings sorted out and for this explosion of passion for me.

Later, she wanted to show me some new jewellery she had made. "I've been working very hard lately," she explained.

"Wow, they're gorgeous." She had laid some of them out on her night table, with all kinds of radiant stones and crystals in various colours. "Where did you find them? They're gorgeous!".

It was at that precise moment that my eyes fell upon this one crystal that looked very familiar. I picked it up to take a closer look. And there it was: Her birthday engraved in it, with a couple letters added, which could only originate from *Freeland*. She must have noticed the huge astonishment written on my face.

"Have you ever heard of a place called *Belleza*?" she asked with a big smile on her face, as she put her loving arms around me. "My house was on the same street as yours." I couldn't believe it and I was totally overwhelmed by this turn of events.

"I stayed there for about six weeks, and then I knew I wanted to be with you. I missed you too much. Being there gave me plenty of time to think. And, living right next to the house you had stayed in, made me think of you each time I passed by. I went in there many times as the couple who lives there now became my friends. I was constantly reminded of you, and I missed you more every day. When people found out where I came from, they all asked about you and Robbie."

"After being transferred back, everyone was still sleeping as I had left them," she continued her story. "I know, the same thing had happened to Robbie and I. Did you meet any of your friends while in *Freeland*?"

"No, I didn't. But I made so many new friends there, you wouldn't believe it. Remember Pepe, the baker? His girlfriend and I became very close friends. She wanted to come back to

Earth, so he decided he would do the same. He found another baker to take over his place. Maybe we can meet up with them sometime.

"That is amazing," I said. "I would love to meet them again."

"After six weeks, I wanted to come back so badly, you can't imagine. And, I also found these stones while there. Eddie took me and others for a few excursions to 'Crystal Valley'. You wouldn't believe how many creative people I met." I hadn't been to 'Crystal Valley', so I was very excited to hear everything about it. "There are many caves filled with clusters, and since noone is greedy, everyone going there takes only a few pieces. And you should have seen the crystal shop there! It's run by some folks from Brazil, and they make all kinds of gorgeous jewellery pieces with those crystals. They have a huge collection. They have gathered all the various crystals that can be found there, and organized a cave tour where visitors could see all of them."

"And, you know what?" It seemed like she had to catch her breath from telling me all these exciting things. "The aliens leave them the list with the birthdays of upcoming *transfers*, and then a few volunteers engrave the phone number into those crystals that each one gets upon arrival."

"And how do the aliens pick them up before giving them to everyone?" I wanted to know.

"They never meet the aliens. The crystals are being picked up while everyone's sleeping. They don't know how the aliens get them to shine in the dark; it's a mystery. Francisco and Amelia, who run the crystal shop there, are very sweet, and I went back to visit them a few times. They've already invited me to go visit them in Brazil. They are absolutely passionate about crystals."

We told each other everything about our time there. It was so precious. Not only was it an answer to my prayers that she could go there, but also something I knew had changed her life, and had apparently made a lot of things clear to her.

"How did you reach out? I mean, was there anything

specific that made you want to go to such a place?"

She was thoughtful for a moment. Then she explained to me that she had gotten quite desperate about her relationship with Tom, especially when she realized that she wasn't that much in love with him and would need to somehow let him know. "The thought of hurting him gave me sleepless nights, and I just wanted so much to get away from this world for a little while. I was getting sick and tired of hurting others and getting hurt, in addition to all that I already feel is wrong in this world. I guess I was ready for that kind of a trip!"

Another lonely traveller had found her way home, I thought.

Chapter 17: As tears go by

A few months later, Anouk and Robbie moved into the neighbouring house closest to mine. By some miracle, it had become vacant recently. They were given the option to rent it and then buy it later if they wanted to. By that time, Birgit had already moved into my house with me. We were all so thrilled to be able to live right next to each other, and Robbie and I would holler over in the morning from our terrace, just like we'd often done in *Freeland*.

By some other miracle, my parents had passed on a financial gift to me, which was just enough to pay back the rest of the credit to the bank. There hadn't been much left to pay as it was a simple house, as was mentioned before. It was such a relief for me! We transformed Birgit's apartment into an art gallery, where I now sold my paintings. Her shop had a large sign over the entrance: 'B and B's jewellery and art gallery.'

My paintings continued to sell well, and with having my credit paid back to the bank, I now needed less money. I decided to quit my job at the office and to dedicate my time solely to painting. Pablo, the owner of the excursion boats, was sad to see me go. He lightened up though when I introduced Anouk to him, who spoke several languages too, and he gave the job to her. She was very thankful for this opportunity. Pablo still wanted my paintings hanging at the office, so I continued supplying him with some of my creations as well.

Time flew by. Jasi had finished her art studies in Madrid by now, and had achieved her masters. She, together with her friend and roommate Lolita, had finally managed to get their long-desired art gallery.

Birgit and I were sitting on a plane, flying over for the grand opening of "Jasmina and Lolita arts". She didn't know we were coming; there must be some surprise elements in life.

She had sent us a printed invitation to the grand opening, so we had the address of the location, and we got there a couple hours prior to the start of the event. I had somewhat of a dislike for large cities, as they seemed just too noisy and busy for me. Maybe because I had lived on a rather quiet island for so long, up in my somewhat secluded little house. We sat down for a coffee near the gallery, watching the people hurrying around.

"At least the Spanish don't hurry quite as much as some other nationalities do," Birgit said with a twinkle in her eye.

I was taking a moment to think about all the miracles that happened in my life since that time when I had reached bottom and Anne had moved out. "Isn't it amazing," I told Birgit, "all the wonderful things that can happen when we reach out?"

"Yes, Bernardo. When you're thankful for the little things, then the big things start happening."

We were looking forward to see Jasi's new paintings. She had brought a few back with her to show us, and they were extraordinary. Birgit would always make sure to take photos of them, as a couple weeks later they might already be sold. Jasi had organized a professional photographer to document her works, as she wanted to publish an art book in the future. Birgit had organised prints of the photos, putting them into frames and hanging them up around our house.

There was a certain sensitivity in Jasi's art that was unique. It was as if each stroke of paint on the canvas was a flower petal from her soul. She had advanced technically a lot during her years of studies, while continuously developing her own style. When some experts would judge her art negatively, saying that it's not what she'd been taught, she wouldn't care. She wanted to be her authentic self in her expression of art, whether others liked it or not. Many art lovers did apparently like it, and her name had become quite known within the local art community. So much so, that a couple of sponsors had helped her with opening the gallery.

Her tender blends and mixes of colours were an

expression of the development of her character, which I had observed over the past years. She had become very mature in her thinking, and we'd had long discussions during her visits about life, our existence, the world, and the society we lived in. Thinking about her paintings, I could literally see her soft colours in my mind. She had a gift of painting nature in a way that made you feel the gentle breeze of the sea, blowing at you right out of the painting, or you could hear the waves splashing ashore, if you wanted to.

Birgit and I were both nervous, since neither of us were used to be in large groups of people, and we wanted to enter before the crowd would stream in. There was quite a long line of people waiting outside the gallery, but they kindly allowed us through, after I explained that I was her father. And so, when the doors opened we went right in, with Jasi looking at us in pleasant surprise.

We fell into each other's arms. "I just wanted to be the first to greet you, my girl!" I exclaimed.

I informed her that we'd be staying for just one night, and right away the girls offered us to stay at their place. We then stood there beside them, helping to greet all their guests. They were of course very interested to meet *el padre*.

The gallery consisted of three exhibition rooms. Most of the paintings were hers, a smaller part from Lolita, and then there was my whole *Freeland collection*. I liked the decor of the place; it was done in the same soft tones that she used in her paintings. It just lulled you into a heavenly atmosphere, and made you want to stay forever. We liked Lolita's paintings too; she used a much more contemporary style, but still noticeably nature-influenced.

There was this one painting from Jasi that caught our attention. She had worked on it last time while home for a visit, but she didn't want us to see it. She had spent some days on that painting down at *the rocks* in Los Cristianos. So here it finally was, hanging on the wall, and one didn't need to be a genius to see that it was Brigit and I sitting on the rocks, both looking out over the ocean towards the sunset, just as we had done so many times over the years. We both shed a tear when we saw it. We clenched each other tightly, staring in awe at this piece of art, as feelings of gratitude came over us for having each other, and for all we'd gone through to get us where we were now.

And not only that, it also made me realize that Jasi had fully accepted the changes that had taken place in our lives, and had moved on with her own, which was something I had been concerned about in the past.

"Your collection matches this place and our paintings so well," Jasi said, as she was showing us around.

Not bad, I thought, *considering that I had never even studied art*. For one second I felt just a little bit proud of myself. Jasi had put price tags under my paintings as well, and she surely had guts for pricing high.

"A lot crappier stuff than yours sells for a lot more, Daddy," she told me, when I questioned the price. I would have never dared to ask that much. But, with time, I learned from her that one who needed to make a living from art shouldn't be too modest, but accepting their value in this world, without becoming arrogant.

I had given her my *Freeland collection* as a gift. It was part of my help to Jasi towards getting started. She loved them so much, and had wondered where I'd gotten those picturesque and divine impressions from. "Does such a place even exist?" she had asked. I had told her that "in art, anything can come into existence."

Wine and *tapas* were being served, and we went to mingle with the crowd, while Jasi and Lolita were kept very busy with all the visitors who wanted to talk to them. When people found out I was her father they were of course very pleased to meet me.

I was surprised to see how well they spoke of Jasi, and what talent she had. Many of the people there seemed to have a rather upper-class background; people who could afford to buy art. I reckoned that many were there not only to look, but also to buy something. *Good for Jasi*, I thought. It was nice that she was now able to sell enough paintings to pay her own bills. Not that I would have had a problem to keep helping her, but it obviously took some financial pressure off, and I felt that life would have other things in store for me now.

Jasi came over and introduced me to some of her friends, telling them that I am the painter, Bernardo. That's how I signed my paintings. A couple of people bought several of my paintings that evening, and Jasi asked me to send some new ones soon.

On our way to their flat I told Jasi: "You seem to be so full of energy and fulfilled!"

"That's true. We've had some marvellous experiences lately. Being able to open my gallery has been a dream come true. Also, Lolita and I have been spending a lot of time going out to nature, which has been essential for a better connection to spiritual energy," she said. "You were the one who got me interested in nature and spirituality. Remember the first meditation we did together under the stars on La Gomera?"

"How could I forget that! I was a very bright occasion during very dark times."

"Well, that meditation we did together had initiated a spiritual search in me that has recently culminated in some wonderful highlights. And sweet mom has continued to give me yoga classes whenever I've visited. I've been able to discover the direction I want to take in my life, and your sample of seeking for simplicity has greatly helped me."

After getting up the next morning we had breakfast together. Birgit and I would be catching a plane back later that day. Lolita needed to go for an appointment early, and we said our goodbyes. I looked around their new flat, at their paintings, including some of mine, and was gibbering over how nicely they had decorated their new home. Then, my eyes fell upon a couple of crystals hanging on the wall.

"Wow, they are gorgeous. Where did you get them from?" She unhooked one of them and handed it over to me.

"Be careful, don't drop it. It's a special gift Lolita and I

163

received." I picked it up carefully and examined it closely. Just taking it in my hand felt like holding something very special; not to speak of the energy it exuberated.

"Good vibes coming from this for sure," I noted. It reminded me of my own crystal I'd received.

"We had someone put it on a necklace, because we like to wear it sometimes. It means a lot to me." I looked at it closer. My eyes widened as I noticed her birthday engraved in it, with a couple additional letters.

"Your phone number?" I asked, as I turned around and looked in her eyes. I saw such warmth and love there.

With a big smile, she said: "In *Bellezza*. Same house as you!"

"Unbelievable! Did you guys go to see the full moon?"

"Nope. We took a hike up in the hills and sat down to meditate, when suddenly some lights came down from the mountain nearby."

"They must have changed tactics then, so that humanity can't catch up with what they're doing."

"Yes! They are smart, and most of all, very loving!" she said, as we were all hugging each other.

And so it was, that yet some more *lonely travellers* had found their way home.

About the author

Sereno Sky is planning on writing yet another continuation of Lonely Traveller at some point in the future. You can stay informed at:

www.serenosky.tumblr.com

Facebook: Sereno Sky

Instagram: lonelytravellerserenosky

For further information, questions or interviews, you may contact Sereno per e-mail at:

serenoskyproductions@outlook.com

"Lonely Traveller" (2014) and "Lonely Traveller Part 2" (2016) are both available on amazon.com

Made in the USA
San Bernardino, CA
21 January 2020